THE RETURN TO Elingale

BILL ROWE

THE RETURN TO ELINGALE

Editorial Production: Diane O'Connell, Write to Sell Your Book, LLC
Cover Design: Lisa Hainline
Layout: Steve Plummer/SPBookDesign
Production Management: Janet Spencer King, Book Development Group

Printed in the United States of American for Worldwide Distribution
ISBN: 978-0-9960489-3-4

Electronic editions:
Mobi ISBN 978-0-9960489-4-1
Epub ISBN: 978-0-9960489-5-8

First Edition

Acknowledgements

With thanks:

To my wife, Sharman, advocate and first reader who lent her unique name to the princess and is now a local celebrity, aka Princess Sharman; to Debbie Neumann, a second reader and inner-city reading teacher that promotes literacy by spending her personal wealth on books so that every child has a fun book to take home and read; and to my patient editor Diane O'Connell and her staff at Write to Sell Your Book for helping me to continue the dream.

Chapter 1

*T*HAND STOOD ON the sandy beach, not far from his home in Elingale, watching the three-masted clipper. Aboard the ship was Lord Creedy, the corrupt overlord of Lapis Lazuli, on his way to Adrianna Island to stand trial.

A gentle wind wafting over the turquoise sea brought the distinct sound of a clanking anchor. It was the final reminder that Thand's first love, Princess Sharman, was also aboard, returning to her father's kingdom.

Neither was happy with parting, but her words "As fast as the wind can carry me, I'll return" had given him hope that they had a future together.

The wind filled the ship's sails, and it began to move away from Elingale. Thand sighed deeply. The people most responsible for helping him lead a successful rebellion were on that ship. He now had to confront two major problems on his own. First: find Baylock, the magician who helped Lord Creedy nearly destroy Elingale. Outdone by the Elwins, Baylock would seek revenge.

Second: lead Elingale out of the past and into the present. Thand had no idea how to make any of this happen, but because he had led the rebellion, the Elwins would expect him to modernize the island.

The Elwins were a mix of several races but mostly elf. This elfin ancestry gave them their pointed ears, their mysterious, blue eyes, and their thick, shiny hair. Most were broad in the shoulders, but six inches shorter than the average human. Despite their compact size, they were strong and tenacious, built to work the land. Unfortunately, no one knew how to govern or operate a business.

Markets, transportation, distribution—all were words that Creedy had used, but Thand had no idea how they worked. Regrettably, he could not expect help from the community. Many of the elders, like his father, had died young. The remainders had been broken in spirit by years of abuse.

Looking out on the horizon, he watched as the *Trident Seas* disappear over the horizon. His shoulders dropped. *What now?*

Overwhelmed by the choices he would have to make, he rubbed his arm several times and then turned for home. At the top of the steep trail he paused to catch his breath. He loved this view. The wide, gently rolling valley flowed from east to west. Planted fields and low stone walls crisscrossed hills of grazing sheep.

The road on which he stood branched into two lanes. They both ran toward the village of Elingale and ended at a modest waterfall that tumbled down the side of the steep hill. A dozen neat houses, built from fieldstone and covered with thatched roofs, formed the village.

He slowly inhaled the sweet air and then followed the path that led to his family's cottage.

Thand stepped inside to find his mother cutting vegetables. She looked up and tilted her head, as if sensing his uneasiness.

"Is everything okay?"

He looked at his frail mother and tried to contain the hatred he had for Creedy. He wished that he could undo the pain she had suffered while locked in his vile dungeon. During her imprisonment, the previously fit, middle-aged lady had transformed into an older woman. She had become hunched, her dark brown hair replaced with gray. The sparkle in her eyes and twenty pounds of weight had been wrung from her while she was held against her will.

Thand wanted to tell his mother everything that was bothering him, but instead he smiled and said, "Everything's good."

He entered his bedroom, but something was amiss. His eyes narrowed. There was a neatly folded piece of paper lying on his bed. *Who put that there?*

He picked up the note and unfolded it. A sudden coldness struck him. The small, neat handwriting looked like it belonged to Baylock. It read, "Look over your shoulder! I don't accept defeat."

Chapter 2

THE WIZARD BAYLOCK knew this day was coming; yet, he was still taken by surprise. He rushed through his lavish home and into the library, slamming the door behind. Towering windows, a fieldstone fireplace, and hundreds of precious books—all of it had to be left behind. His nostrils flared as he locked the door. He wanted to hurt someone, to see blood. *These accursed Elwins! How did those uneducated sod farmers outmaneuver me?*

The powerful warlock was filled with bitterness and resentment. Through some unknown power, the villagers of Elingale had succeeded in destroying his magic spell. No one had ever dared to challenge his mystical powers before. That act of defiance would not be forgotten or forgiven.

Baylock's vast home was positioned near the edge of a steep cliff located in the northern part of Lapis Lazuli. Here, he made a very comfortable living selling destructive potions and spells. Lord Creedy, his most valued customer, had just been arrested for kidnapping, abuse, and numerous other crimes against the Elwins. Now they were coming for him. Why? He was simply doing his job. Guilt by association? A poor excuse to hunt a man down.

Several chairs and tables were scattered about the room, but nothing substantial for barricading the door. He hurried to his prized marble sculpture, a jeweled sword protruding from a solid rock. Hastily, he depressed the red gemstone on the sword's pommel. A faint click followed, and then a quiet sigh. The floor dropped an inch. The cover slid back silently, releasing a pale yellow vapor that rose from the inky pit and spread across the floor.

He glanced over his shoulder one last time before rushing down the hidden stairway.

A pungent, sulfurous smell wrinkled his nose and stung his eyes as he descended into the deserted laboratory. At the bottom of the stairs, he picked up a narrow tube hanging on a post and shook it several times. A soft, bluish-green light dispersed the darkness. Holding the stick high, he scanned the room one last time.

Empty. The jars, flasks, and tools of his trade had already been packed and sent ahead to a secret location. But his prized creatures were still here, and they had to be saved.

He rushed to the iron door that was built into the stone wall. On the other side, resting upside down, were the bohes. These bat-like creatures were his greatest achievement to date. They had almost succeeded in turning Elingale into a smoldering heap of the ashes.

The bohes resembled giant bats with a five-foot wingspan, but that's where the comparison ended. Through experimentation, he had merged the speed and agility of a bat with the fiery ferociousness of a dragon. It was a formidable creature that responded to no one's command but his. Satan, the rebellious leader of the dark underworld, would be proud of Baylock's accomplishment.

A noise made him look back toward the steps. *An intruder!* His heart pounded like a hammer against an anvil. A large rat scurried across the ring of bluish-green light and into a corner. He let out a heavy sigh. The stairs remained empty.

Returning to his effort of freeing the bohes, he fumbled through the ring of keys on his belt. *Where's that key?* Then he reached into his pockets and uttered a profanity. There was nothing there but a piece of lint.

"Gotterslamit," he cursed. "I don't have time for this!"

His arm muscles tightened. A flash of light jumped from his fingertips, and the lock shattered into a thousand pieces.

Light-headed from the energy drain, he paused. *Get your focus back or the next sound of keys will be from a jailer.* He covered his mouth and nose, aware of what was waiting inside. Then, taking a deep breath, he yanked on the handle.

Humid, rank air rushed out, triggering a reflexive gag. He coughed several times. Then, waving his hand in front of his face, he stepped through the doorway. The sleek, bat-like monsters were hanging quietly from the ceiling.

Ducking low, hoping to avoid their deadly, barbed tails, he passed beneath the bohes and into a rear passageway. He paused a moment to wipe his feet and then continued into a murky tunnel. A brief way down, he turned left, and a slender rectangle of light appeared in the distance. *Freedom!* He ran the last hundred yards to the exit.

A pain shot through his chest, warning him to slow down. But each minute of delay increased the chance of imprisonment.

He paused at the rust-coated door to catch his breath. Chirping noises came echoing through the tunnel. *What's disturbed them?* He pulled on the door, but it didn't budge. The salt air had corroded the hinges.

He whispered a simple incantation: "Unbind the way." Slowly, like a rusty coffin lid, the door opened. Blazing light flooded in and blinded him. For a moment, he was paralyzed. White and black circles were all that he could see. Then, fresh air rushed into the tunnel and cleared the rank air. As his vision cleared, the blinding light faded to blue skies. The sea air and warm sun lifted his spirits. *Almost home.*

Baylock moved out to the pier and saw his single-mast sloop bobbing gently alongside the pier. The forty-foot sailboat was patiently waiting, ready to be freed from its tether and sail him to his new residence. After three years of construction, his new house was ready. *House*, he laughed to himself. *No, fortress.*

He went back to the cave's doorway and placed two fingers on his lips. A piercing whistle shot down the tunnel and summoned the bohes. Immediately, a high frequency vibration rushed through the tunnel, and a fluttering, flapping frenzy followed. The wizard crouched low as the bohes raced inches above him, their forked, rat-like tails barely missing his head. The downdraft from the creatures' massive wings stirred the dark hair on his head. When the last bohe had left the cave, he stood and watched the winged creatures fly in a drunken line toward the east.

He walked toward the sloop, grinding his teeth and mumbling, "How did the Elwins find a way to reverse my spell? Who helped them? Well, it doesn't matter. Before long I'll return, and this time I won't lose."

Chapter 3

SUDDENLY THE BEDROOM door burst open and Thand's younger brother, Eschon, ran in. Panting hard and waving his arms, he called out, "Hurry! You must see what we've found."

There was no mistaking that Eschon was Thand's brother. He was two years younger and one inch less in height, but both shared the same silver-blue eyes and impish smiles.

Thand quickly stuffed the note in his pocket and turned toward his brother. "Maybe later. Too much to do right now."

"You need to see this to believe it. Get moving!" Eschon was not normally this dramatic. He tended to be even-tempered like his older brother. "I mean it. Come now!" Eschon said. Then he turned and ran out the door.

Thand didn't need another distraction, but there was nothing he could do regarding the note except tell Eschon. He went to the doorway and yelled, "What's the rush? Can't this wait? I have something important to tell you."

Eschon was skipping sideways down the path, waving Thand on. "No, it can't. You must see what Glundel and Dayv found."

Thand caught up to his brother, but his eyes narrowed when he saw that the beauty of the grotto hill was lost to a pile of dirt.

Elingale was such a well-ordered village. The clutter and confusion of the crowd was annoying.

"What's the big deal? Someone is always finding something new," said Thand.

"They've found a single bone bigger than me. We don't know what to think," Eschon gushed. "Someone guessed it's a dragon bone."

Thand raised his eyebrows and walked toward the object for a closer look.

The crowd parted. They were always happy to see Thand. If anyone could figure this out, it would be him.

Thand tilted his head to one side. Eschon's excitement was well placed. Knuckles on either end of the object suggested that it was some type of bone. It was as broad as a tree trunk and longer than an Elwin. He stooped down and rubbed his hand along the gray bone. There were a few cracks in the surface and a chip where the shovel had struck it.

His skin began to tingle. "Incredible."

"And it's just one bone," Eschon said eagerly. "I can't imagine the actual size of this thing."

Thand stood up. "If it's genuine, then we finally have proof that dragons exist. I can't wait to tell the skeptics."

"Like Princess Sharman?" Eschon said as he bumped Thand's shoulder.

"Yes," he said. "Especially her."

He tried to stand the bone upright, but it wouldn't budge. So he lay down alongside it.

Eschon gave a long whistle. "It's at least a foot longer than you."

Thand jumped up and brushed the dirt from his clothes. "It looks like the leg bone of a horse—except it's ten times bigger."

Eschon tilted his head. "I wonder how the dragon died. Was it shot out of the sky or killed by another dragon?"

"Good question," said Thand. "How would you slay a dragon? Our puny arrows couldn't kill anything that big."

Eschon crouched and ran his hand along the bone. "It had to be gigantic." Then he jumped up quickly. "Come on, kin; let's go to the mansion library. Maybe Creedy left something interesting that can help us figure it out."

Thand hesitated. He needed to talk to Eschon about the note, but there were too many ears listening. He looked one more time at the bone and his stomach fluttered. *Mysterious notes, dragon bones, what else can happen today?*

"Good idea. Let's go."

Just as Thand was about to leave, one of the village elders hobbled over. He was about forty years old. Wrinkled brown skin and a bowed back made him look sixty. "Many of the older people don't like this digging," he said in an irritated voice. "They fear you have dishonored a dragon burial place. We think that one might return to seek vengeance."

Thand gave the elder a reassuring smile and said, "It's not likely that a dragon will return. That bone has been buried for a very long time."

"But still, we're worried. Ya know, Lord Creedy would keep us safe."

Blood rushed to Thand's head. "What! You want Creedy back? After all he's done to us?"

The elder took a step back. "Well, I guess not. But we need to know what's going to happen to us. No one's in charge now. Who's going to protect us? We're old and need to be reassured that we'll be okay. Maybe you could have a meeting so we can figure this out."

Thand tugged on his ear and calmed down. "Okay, I understand. I'll hold a town meeting in the next few days."

Chapter 4

*T*HAND AND ESCHON stepped timidly through the door of Creedy's mansion. It felt strange to just open the door and walk in. Very few Elwins had ever been inside the great house, and the few that had were usually sent there for punishment.

Thand saw his brother's eyes widened to the size of walnuts. rooms, the leather chairs, and the cherry-panel walls seemed to puzzle him.

"Amazing isn't it? You can come back later and look around," said Thand. "Follow me."

Inside the library, Thand quickly located his favorite book of knowledge. It was called an encyclopedia, and it contained information on all kinds of subjects. He didn't understand many of the topics yet, but he knew if he kept using it, he would improve. Flipping through the pages, Thand soon found what he'd been hunting for. He waved impatiently for his brother to come over.

"Look, Eschon. This is excellent. It says that dragons *are* descendants of dinosaurs, not *were*. That means they still exist. Now I have at least one answer for the town meeting. And here, on the next page, is the bone structure of a dragon. The humerus bone looks like the one you found."

"The drawing looks very complicated. "And by the way, what does descendent mean?"

"Good question. A month ago, all of these books would have only been good for starting a fire. But now we can read. Look how much we've discovered since then. No wonder Creedy and Baylock were keeping us illiterate."

Thand looked out the window toward Elingale. "I wish we had captured Baylock. I'm afraid he'll come back and try to get even."

"I hope his boat sank," Eschon said sharply.

"If he comes back, we always have Enunciation. He's a much better wizard. Now, go over to the shelf by the door and look for a book with the word *dictionary* on the side. Then bring it to me."

"Dictionary? What's a dictionary?"

"It's a famous book, very important if you want to become a good reader. It's like having your own teacher with you all of the time."

Eschon found the heavy book, brought it to the table, and then dropped it with a *thunk*. "Now what?"

"A dictionary explains the meaning of words. Let's say you're reading and you see a word that you don't understand, like *descendant*. You go to your dictionary and start searching. The words are listed in alphabetical order." Thand paused and looked up at his brother. "You do understand the meaning of alphabetical order, right? *A, B, C, D, E—*"

"Of course," Eschon said curtly. "That's one of the first things we learned."

Thand wrote *descendant* on a piece of paper and handed it to his brother. "Okay. Here's how it's spelled. Now, flip through the pages until you find the *D* section. Then look down for *DE* words. Add the *S* and the *C*. Keep adding letters until you find *descendant.* Then read the description. It will explain the meaning of the word."

"That sounds like a lot of work."

"If your thick head absorbs the meaning of the word, you'll only have to do it once. Just remember, the more words you understand, the easier it is to read."

Eschon opened the dictionary to the section that began with the letter *D*, and then began the alphabetical search.

"Look, here it is. *De-scend-ant*: A person or animal that is descended from a specific ancestor; an offspring," Eschon said, pleased with himself. "We need to tell Scribe about this book. He could use the dictionary to teach the children a new word every day."

"Good idea, but it's not just about reading. The more words you understand, the better you'll be able to follow a conversation."

An idea came to Thand. "Eschon, you know Enunciation is said to be a wizard, but what's a wizard actually do? Look that word up in your dictionary."

Eschon turned the book to the W's. "This should be easy, I know how to spell *wizard*." He flipped the pages until he found *WI*, then moved down past the words *withstand, witness, wives,* until he found *wizard.* "Here it is," he said with a crisp nod. "It says that the word means wise one. 'A wizard is usually a solitary practitioner of magic born with the exceptional ability to control the forces of nature. His vast knowledge of the natural world allows him to rearrange the energies into spells and incantations.' Wow, that sounds exciting. I wonder if I could learn that."

"Maybe you'll get to meet him someday, and then you can ask him for yourself."

Eschon sat up straight. "That would be great!"

Thand stood. "I wish Duvin hadn't asked for a meeting. I'm not ready to answer all their questions."

Eschon's eyes furrowed. "Cancelling the town meeting would be a bad idea Thand. These people look up to you and expect a strategy. You're our leader, so you better come through."

Thand clenched his jaw. "Gotterslamit! Why always me?"

Chapter 5

As Baylock hurried to his boat, the bohes disappeared into the horizon. How had he been manipulated into abandoning his own house? What made these Elwins different? He remembered seeing the Elwin boy named Thand leaving Creedy's field. Thand had projected a surprising image of authority for an upstart.

As Baylock recalled, it was Thand who had befriended the girl from Adrianna Island, a teenaged princess named Sharman. She was smart to understand that the Elwins' illiteracy was keeping them from improving their lives. The villagers had learned quickly, absorbing their lessons like the desert sands in a rainstorm. He heard that his old nemesis, the Wizard Enunciation, had joined with them. He could handle the Elwins, but Enunciation was a powerful enemy. He would try to keep him out of the fight.

He looked to the east and swept his arm out toward the sea. "Don't worry my red-eyed beasts. This backwoods island was always too small for my ambitions. Fly on to your new home. We'll return later to make them pay."

Boom! echoed across the water.

Baylock flinched at the thunderous sound coming from the

cliff top. The soldiers had arrived and tripped the magical ward that he'd placed on the front door.

He hurried down the wharf, released the mooring lines, and jumped on the boat. As it drifted quietly away, he pulled on the mainsail rigging. Hand over hand. The pulleys squeaked in protest. Then, just as the half-raised sail began to fill with wind, the line jammed.

"Not now," he shouted as he jerked on the rope and kicked the mast.

The angry yank only made the knot tighter. Shaking his head, he climbed the mast to unravel the tangle. He wrapped one arm around the mast, leaving only one hand free to deal with the knot. Clumsily, he fought the snarled rope.

He was high up the mast, and his weight changed the boat's center of gravity. The ship began leaning heavily to one side. Capsizing was a real danger. He shifted his weight, trying to correct the balance. A few tense moments passed as he swung back and forth, still fighting to free the line. Finally, the knot came loose. He looked ahead and checked the position of the drifting boat. *Breaking waves! A submerged reef.* He had to get to the helm and steer away from it or the boat would be crushed against the jagged coral.

He was ten feet above the deck, but he jumped. Just then, a swell caused the boat to lift, and his ankle twisted on impact. He rolled to the edge of the deck, clutching his leg and shrieking in pain. Time was running out, so he crawled across the deck on his elbows. Then, with a great effort, he pulled himself up to reach the ship's wheel. The breaking surf was straight ahead. He spun the wheel toward starboard. There was a sudden jolt. Wood cracked and splintered as the boat's hull raked across the razor-sharp coral.

He looked over the portside and cursed as large pieces of wood drifted by. When the reef was cleared, he tied off the rudder and hobbled below deck to check for damage

Thunk. He'd forgotten to duck his head.

"Son-of-ashade! That hurt." The pain amplified his anger. "Bedamn those Elwins! I'm going to make them pay."

He touched his forehead gingerly. A bleeding lump was rapidly forming.

With his hand resting on the top of his head, he made a careful inspection of the interior but found no leaks. Still, the planking had been weakened. If the waves became too strong, a seam could open up and send him to the bottom. He staggered back to the helm and reset the wheel. Then, calculating the distance to his new home, he took a deep breath and hoped the boat would stay afloat.

Chapter 6

PRINCESS SHARMAN STOOD at the ship's rail and looked back longingly on Elingale. Her long, auburn hair fluttered in the breeze as small teardrops fell from her green eyes. Already, she was missing the Elwins, especially Thand.

A gentle breeze filled the canvas, and calm waves parted at the bow, leaving a foamy wash. All of the *Trident Seas'* sails were hoisted, marking the beginning of the three-day journey to Adrianna Island.

She recalled the past several months. The journey had begun when she left home, Adrianna Island, with her Uncle Warmund. They had been traveling aboard the merchant ship *Odyssey* on an adventure to explore new lands. It had been the princess' first time away from home, and she was in high spirits.

The excitement turned to fear on the second day when out of nowhere a pirate ship appeared and fired on the *Odyssey*. Understanding the fate of a young girl captured by pirates, Uncle Warmund rushed to her cabin and broke the window out. Explaining that there was no other choice, he placed her inside a sea chest, closed the lid, and then tossed it overboard.

The currents carried her to Lapis Lazuli where she met Thand

and Eschon. With no means of return, the boy's mother, Grace, welcomed her into their home.

Within days, the princess learned that the boys could not read or write. Their master, Lord Creedy, had forbidden any form of education. She explained the advantages of literacy, and they agreed it was worth angering Creedy. Several weeks later, Creedy learned that the Elwins had started a school. He retaliated by employing the magician, Baylock, to create a spell that destroyed their ability to read and write. But they had some magic of their own and eventually defeated Baylock and Creedy. At present, Lord Creedy was here, in the *Trident Seas'* brig, returning to Adrianna Island to pay for his crimes.

Late in the afternoon, the ship began to curve toward the sinking sun. The princess' eyebrows furrowed when she realized that her home island was in the opposite direction. Curious about the change, she hurried across the deck toward the captain's cabin. Jumping ropes and avoiding hardworking sailors, she arrived at the doorway. The varnished cabin door was solid oak. She had been informed by the first mate, Oden, that a one-way glass portal had been added for the captain's convenience. She inspected her reflection in the glass. Pushing a loose strand of hair behind her ear, she drew in a deep breath, raised her fist, and knocked.

Captain Boreas was an intimidating man, square built like the ship. He strived for perfection and expected the same from everyone who sailed under his command. An improperly set bone was responsible for his limp, but anyone who mistook his lame walk for a weakness was a fool.

"Present yourself," the captain barked.

Princess Sharman put on her best smile and walked in.

"What can I do for ya, lass?" a baritone voice inquired from behind a desk.

She walked toward him and performed a short bow, playing to his vanity. "I realize I'm not as smart as you, but I am familiar with direction. And my sense of bearing tells me we are not headed home to Adrianna Island."

"I always knew you were smart girl. Recognizing direction is extremely important in the sailor's life," he said, tapping the North Star tattoo on the crown of his bald head.

A chuckle escaped as she recalled the story of the inked image. On the evening of his promotion to captain, his former crewmates had thrown him a party. It was wild and boisterous, even by sailor standards. He woke the next morning with a throbbing head and little memory of the celebration. But when he stared bleary-eyed into the mirror that morning, a Polaris star was tattooed on his bald head.

"Maybe we can make ya a good sailor, then a captain. What da'ya think?" said the captain merrily.

"I'll just stick to being a princess," she said, performing a princess-perfect curtsy.

It was his turn to laugh. "Now, why are you really here?"

"I know you don't like to be questioned, but why are we turning away from Adrianna Island?"

"Your father—excuse me, King Treutlen—gave me orders to search the nearby islands for your Uncle Warmund."

Her hand flew to her chest. "Ripers! Thank you. That's the best reason in the world. I just know we're going to find him."

Boreas was in a rare, cheerful mood. She took a chance and kissed his forehead.

He blushed. "Perhaps we will. But before ya get too excited, remember it's a big ocean. Locating him might be as hard as finding a jug of water in the desert."

She bounced on her toes. "But I'm sure we will. He's talked to me in dreams."

"Well, dreams come from the spirit world, ya know, the land of the dead. So that's maybe not a good sign."

"I don't know if that's true, but that's not a reason to give up."

Too many times she had felt like it was her fault that her uncle was missing. As if she had done something wrong by surviving the pirate attack. What if she hadn't been with him on the ship? Maybe the assault would have never happened. Maybe if her uncle hadn't had to worry with her, he would have been able to save himself. Maybe the sailors were right—girls on ships were bad luck.

Shifting slightly in his chair, Boreas said, "Assuming that Warmund doesn't come to me in a dream and order me to stop searching, we'll hunt for him for the next several days. However, ya must be sensible and prepare yarself for the other possibility."

Putting her hands on her hips, she said, "I will not be sensible, and you're not going to spoil my excitement."

She walked out to the ship's starboard rail and looked into the evening sky. The new moon, which cast no light, allowed the evening stars to sparkle like ice crystals. She closed her eyes and remembered the adage that the new moon was a symbol of restoration, a return of something to a former condition. Hopefully, the mythology was true and her uncle would be returned to her. To reinforce her longing, she made a wish and sent it to a star.

That night she drifted off to sleep with a smile on her face. But in the middle of the night, she began to mumble.

"Uncle Warmund, I'm so glad to see you. Where have you been?"

"Shhh, pirates have taken over the ship."

She sat up slowly and pulled the blankets away, surprised to see that she was fully dressed.

"Am I dreaming? Why are you holding your sword like that?"

Just then the door burst open, and a scar-faced man jumped inside, swinging his sword.

"Who are you?" she asked in a dreamy voice, but her words were lost in the clang of clashing steel.

She watched her uncle struggle as the pirate backed him across the room. Then, with a flick of the wrist, her uncle's sword flew from his hand as Warmund charged, but the pirate grabbed him by the shirt and hurled him through the window.

When morning came, the nightmare was a fuzzy memory. She dressed and went up to the main deck. Already, the day was stifling. Thick, moist air blanketed her body like a shroud. It was going to be the kind of blistering day when the weather could change quickly. The clouds were growing vertical—the first sign of a thunderstorm.

She scouted the upper deck and saw Oden, her friend and the ship's first mate. He had wide shoulders and strong arms, and he was about eight years older than she. He was rolling up a map and walking toward the stern when she called his name.

Oden turned and smiled as she ran across the deck and then up the stairs. In her childish enthusiasm, she pecked him on his cheek and said, "We're going to find my uncle."

"Yes. I received the change of plans yesterday. I've plotted a course for the nearest island. We should arrive sometime tomorrow morning if the wind holds up."

Then she pointed to the tall gray clouds and asked about the possibility of a storm.

"It's too early to tell. But yes, it looks like one's brewing. Have you ever been on a ship during a thunderstorm?"

"No. Should I be worried?"

Oden looked at the gathering clouds. "Yes."

Chapter 7

PRINCESS SHARMAN WOKE with a sense of calm and ease. She felt confident that today they were going to find Uncle Warmund. Everything seemed to be right. The wind had been steady all night, and they expected to reach the first island on time. The storm that had developed the day before had stayed to the south and left them alone. It had been interesting to watch it from a safe distance. The roiling clouds, the flashes of lightning, and the delayed sound of thunder kept her at the ship's rail for over an hour.

She opened her sea chest. *I want to look good today. Never know who I'll meet, and I want Uncle Warmund to see me looking well. The black slacks look good.* A white, scoop-neck tunic followed and then a leather bodice that had to be cinched around her waist. After lacing up her black boots, she pulled a brush quickly through her hair and left the room.

On deck, pink sky replaced the black as the transformation of night to day continued. "Land ho," someone bellowed from the crow's nest. Sharman hurried to the rail and caught sight of a long, dark mass on the horizon. A clear sky silhouetted an island that the charts had labeled Raintree Island. Thin, wispy, gray clouds traced back to a ten-thousand-foot mountain peak.

It wasn't long before they caught sight of a lush rain forest running along the coastline. The base of the mountain swept into the sea and then curved back toward the island like a hook. If the water was deep enough, the ship would have a safe place to anchor and allow them to explore. They rounded the point and discovered a natural harbor. Except for a few tropicbirds and seagulls, the island appeared deserted.

"Furl the sails," ordered the captain. "Looks like good harbor."

A sailor on the yardarm muttered to his mate, "Peaceful and serene is not what it seems. Mark my words. Trouble is hidden on that island."

While anchoring duties were performed, Oden prepared a landing party. Several men lined up, hoping to be chosen. Princess Sharman stepped alongside the men, expecting to be selected. Oden rolled his eyes.

The look on his face made her angry. She folded her arms across her chest. "Have you forgotten the courage it took to defeat Baylock and Lord Creedy? I'm not a weak and helpless child. Don't try to exclude me, Oden. I'm going with you to help search for my uncle. Besides, you'll need someone who can make rational decisions."

He shook his head and sighed. "Trying to protect you from yourself is impossible. You can come, but remember who's in charge."

It didn't take long to row across the tranquil bay, but just as the boat touched the beach two men appeared from behind a sand dune.

Oden attempted to climb out of the boat and greet the men, but a stocky man pulled out his pistol. "What yuh want? Why yuh here? Who dis wuhman?"

"We'd like to speak to the person in charge," the princess said politely.

The second man pointed his pistol at Oden and ordered him

out. Oden jumped over the side into a foot of water and waited. Sharman stood and nervously plucked at her clothes. The second man nodded toward her. She put her hand on the gunwale and vaulted over the side, landing with a splash.

"Dey stay," he said harshly, pointing at the oarsmen. "Only yu two."

Oden told the men to wait in the boat, but listen for any signs of trouble. Then he took the princess' hand and together they followed the strong man up a steep hill and into the lush jungle. Vines as thick as rope hung from the trees. Giant plants with leaves larger than any man crowded the smaller plants for the limited sunlight.

The princess looked around nervously, jumping at each new sound. In minutes the dense vegetation had swallowed them.

Under the jungle's damp canopy it was cooler. Numerous ferns and tree fungus combined to make the air smell dank. A few steps in, she noticed an eerie quiet. Instinctively, she hunched over and searched her surroundings. Her movements became slow and deliberate, as if an ambush lay in wait.

As the sunshine faded into dim shafts of light, the princess thought that leaving the safety of the ship had been a bad idea. Their firearms had been left onboard because the captain didn't want the reconnaissance party to appear hostile. Oden had reluctantly agreed but had wisely refused to part with his sword.

The princess looked at Oden's blade. *Why didn't I bring something to protect myself?* But even if she had, she wasn't trained to defend herself.

A half of a mile into the jungle, they came into a clearing where two bamboo houses had been built several feet off the ground. The roofs were thatched with dried banana leaves. One, the largest of the buildings, resembled a badly built tavern. The other shanty looked like a house slowly being swallowed by vines and tall grass. The front wall of the tavern was divided in two parts. The upper half was hinged and pulled up to make an awning. A countertop had been built across the lower half, making it easy to pass food or drinks.

Three men were seated on barstools with pewter mugs in their hands. They watched every move the strangers made. Sharman felt like she was being inspected, and she checked her clothing to see if something might be exposed. One man leaned over to the others and whispered something, causing a coarse laugh.

The princess rubbed her upper arm and looked behind to see if the path was clear. It crossed her mind that these men might belong to the pirate crew that had attacked her uncle's ship. Oden seemed to sense her anxiety and put his arm around her shoulder, pulling her close to his side. His other hand twitched on the pommel of his sword. They both knew that the odds were against them if a fight broke out.

Two mahogany-skinned men stood up and walked away from their seats, making room for Oden and the princess. The third man, with coffee-colored skin, remained seated and stared at them as if making a decision. When the evaluation seemed complete, the man stood, took off his black tricorn hat, and bowed deeply, making a sweeping gesture.

"My name ah Cayman," he said in a deep, mellow voice, "Ow can me be of help?"

The accent in his speech suggested that he was not from any local island; more likely, he was of the people who lived in the southern hemisphere.

He was tall, with twisted, matted coils of coarse hair dangling beneath a red-head scarf. As if for decoration, two rope-like braids of hair hung on either side of his head. These strands were dyed red and woven with colorful beads. His muscular chest was partly covered by a black leather vest. His pant legs were cut off at the knees, exposing an ugly, jagged scar.

When no one answered his question, Cayman smiled weakly and pointed at Oden's sword.

"Nuh need fah weapons here, sah."

"Just a precaution," Oden said. "You never know what kind of feral creatures may be roaming these islands."

Cayman laughed, pulled out his sword, and expertly slashed an *X* into the air. "Yuh are correct, sah. Dere are dangerous tings upon dis island, but you're safe in dis village."

"Look, *Cayman* was it? I'm having trouble understanding your words. Don't you speak the common language?"

"Me speak your language. Du yuh speak mine?" he said with a smirk.

"I only understand a few words."

"Ahh, then I will show yuh my superior language skills and switch to your dialect."

He smiled warmly at Princess Sharman as he returned his jewel-handled sword to its scabbard.

"Let me provide you a drink," Cayman said perfectly, lightly touching the princess' elbow.

Her shoulders suddenly dropped, and her balled fists relaxed as the charm of this rakish man took hold. Oden rolled his eyes. The man looked like a pirate, smelled like a pirate, and was most likely a pirate.

"Don't touch her," barked Oden.

Ignoring the outburst, Cayman poured two drinks from a bottle and passed the cups to his guests. The liquid was clear but had a strong, pungent odor. Oden snatched his glass and sniffed at it, then took a gulp, made a face, and slammed the cup back on the table, as if performing some male ritual. Princess Sharman saw that it was safe to drink and did the same. But before she could swallow, her eyes grew large and her throat constricted. She shook violently and coughed out the coarse liquid in a messy spray.

"What is this?" she gagged. "Give me some water."

"Why, it's just a cup of rum. We distill it here, on de island."

"I'm sorry, Princess," Oden stammered. "It never occurred to me that you hadn't tasted rum before. We sailors drink it like water. In fact, there would be a rebellion if the sailors didn't get their daily grog."

Oden turned to Cayman and gave him a sour look. "You should have told her that rum was in her cup."

"Me! Why didn't yuh?"

Oden cleared his throat and then scowled, "What exactly is it that you do on this island?"

Cayman's face tightened. "Who are yuh to come to my island and start asking questions? It is I who wants to know why yuh are here."

Oden's voice rose. "Not to drink your lousy rum."

"If yuh don't like my hospitality, yuh can leave."

Princess Sharman jumped to her feet, looking from face to face. "Please, restrain yourselves, both of you." She focused her gaze on Cayman. "We're not here to start trouble. We're searching for a man, about forty years old. He may have washed up on this island. He was on a merchant ship many months ago when it was attacked and set on fire by pirates. He's my uncle, and I'm here to take him home."

"I'm sorry, miss," Cayman said sincerely. "We have no strangers on dis island." Then he looked at Oden and sneered, "Except dis man."

Oden clenched his jaw. "Then you won't mind if we walk around the village and ask a few questions."

"Just be gone before dark."

Chapter 8

PRINCESS SHARMAN AND Oden left the tavern shack and followed the trail a half of a mile into the jungle. Oden kept looking back anxiously.

Finally, the princess put her hand on his shoulder, stopping him. "What's bothering you, Oden? You've been acting like a bully."

Oden said, "I don't trust that guy Cayman. He reminds me of someone I'd rather forget."

"And who would that be? You?"

Oden cleared his throat. "Let's forget it. The past is past."

Her eyes widened as she made the connection. "A pirate! You? No, you've always been kind and protective."

Oden walked away briskly, clearly wanting to avoid the topic.

She caught up to him but decided to change the subject. "Wouldn't it be nice if we had Thand with us?"

"He has a lot to sort out now that he's taking over Lord Creedy's role. But he'll succeed. Just look what he's done already. "

Suddenly, she stopped. Sucking in a quick breath, she pointed down. Her voice raised several octaves. "Oden, look! How did that get there? It doesn't make sense."

Oden stopped in midstride and looked down into the deep

valley. Nestled among the ferns and jungle plants was a perfectly intact, three-mast ship.

A moment passed in silence as both tried to solve the mystery.

Slowly, a smile crossed Oden's face. "The cleverness is remarkable. Look to the stern—the back of the ship," he said. "There's a narrow river, more like a canal. It follows the valley floor back out to the bay. They must have floated the ship in here, probably using mules to pull it along."

"Over there," the princess pointed excitedly. "Look hard. They're concealed pretty well."

There were four cottages built from wooden planks with green, moss-covered roofs. A blacksmith shop was near and some type of mill sat alongside a waterfall that fed into the canal. Smoke drifted from chimneys while chickens scratched and pigs scoured the ground for anything edible.

Oden laughed impulsively. "How ingenious! This is a ship repair facility hidden in the jungle. Anyone sailing into the bay would never know this place exists. Pirates wouldn't know that a boat was here for the taking—or a village for the plundering. But if by chance the hamlet was discovered, the people could simply fade into the jungle."

A sharp sound, like wood snapping, came from behind their backs. Both turned quickly to face a broad-shouldered man with large, calloused hands. He clenched a thick club, raised as if ready for a fight.

"I hope you're looking to repair a ship," the man said with a wavering smile.

"No," Oden said a little too harshly.

"Then you must be looking for trouble."

Oden balled his hands and shifted to a wide stance.

Princess Sharman jumped between them. "But it's nice to

know that there is a place like this if I should have trouble in the future."

Then Sharman placed her hand on the man's chest. "We're looking for my uncle. I'd normally describe him as a tall, heavyset man, but he's been missing so long he could be any size. He probably has a beard."

The man's face softened when he realized they were friendly. "I'm sorry, miss; sometimes those men out there in the shacks sometimes bring trouble. Unfortunately, no one fitting that description has been seen around here."

Her shoulders slumped. "Are you sure?"

"I'm sure. Nothing happens on this island without me knowing about it. Maybe he landed on another island. Skull Island is the nearest."

By now, half a dozen villagers had gathered around, listening to the conversation. A woman with a black leather apron hanging around her neck and a blacksmith's hammer in one hand spoke up.

"Skull Island. About a day's sail from here. And don't think it's called that 'cause of a sandy beach with a few bleached bones scattered about. It's named that 'cause of a cave that's shaped like a giant human skull. Pure evil."

She looked around at the group. "Em I right?"

The villagers nodded in agreement. Oden smiled and turned to the princess. "People tend to exaggerate. When we leave here, we'll investigate for ourselves."

"No!" the anxious villagers shouted in unison.

The blacksmith woman shook her hammer as she spoke each word. "You don't want to go there." She stepped closer to Sharman. "If your friend washed up on Skull Island, he is already dead."

The princess' head jerked back. "Dead! What do you mean?"

The woman tapped the side of her head. "Are ya daft?" She

turned her head sideways and looked up at her husband. "Don't she hear good? Dead means dead!"

The man placed his beefy hand on his wife's arm and then pulled her back. "Calm down, Smithy. Your words are scaring her." He looked back to the princess. "We should tell you there're lots of snakes slithering around that island."

"Snakes are rarely a problem," said the princess, fixing a stare on the woman. "Most of them try to avoid humans and are only dangerous if cornered."

"Your fancy clothes tell me how much you know about snakes," she sneered. "How 'bout you ever seen one called a two-step viper, with a large triangle head and a bite that's instant death. Well, they're all over Skull Island. Instead of crawling from noise, they're attracted to vibration. And when the viper spots prey, it raises up about two feet and *sssingss* a mesmerizing siren's song. The snake strikes the dazed victim with its poisonous bite, and within two steps, you're dead." She nodded her head sharply on the last two words.

The princess' brows drew together, as if doubting the story. "Singing snakes? I never heard of such a thing."

"That's 'cause dead men can't tell stories. But if that don't scare you away, then there's a deadly spider. It's the size of a large dog, with bristly, gray and tan hair that blends perfectly with the underbrush.

"Mactabilis," the princess whispered with fear. "I know that spider. Thand has told me about that awful creature."

"Hey, Braun, she's gett'n'it." The villagers chuckled but she continued. "So, you know it has multiple red eyes that look everywhere at once. Eight legs and a pincher like a claw. It don't let go. The thing kills its victim by spitting some sticky purple venom onto it."

The woman spit on the ground for emphasis and continued. "The poison slowly dissolves the poor creature and makes it more digestible. It's just best you stay away."

She looked over at her husband, "Ya think she knows now, Braun?"

"That's the thing that killed Thand's father," she said to Oden.

The broad-shouldered man with calloused hands spoke up again.

"If somehow you get past the snakes, there's the Sentry Plants that grow near the cave. Body heat causes the plants' spiked leaves to rub together. It makes a loud clicking sound like big crickets. They know you're coming."

A man with huge biceps and soot on his face spoke up. "When the moon is bright, we see dragons in the sky."

The princess raised her palm toward the man. "Please, not that story. They don't exist."

"Says you," he snapped, clearly annoyed by her response.

Before an argument started over the existence of dragons, Oden thanked the villagers and turned the princess around. They hiked back whike alked back the trail toward the ship.

"Not the friendliest people I ever met," she noted. "What do you think about Skull Island?"

"Let's hope it's just folklore and no more," said Oden.

"The spider is real. The dragon is nonsense. I'm not sure about the rest."

He put his hand on her back to hurry her along. "We'll soon find out."

Chapter 9

*T*HAND WALKED TO the beach and found the log where Princess Sharman had sat the first day that they met. He remembered her coughing up water as she tried to thank Eschon and him for saving her life. The near-tragedy marked the beginning of their unlikely relationship.

The sounds of the gently lapping waves were soothing. He could have sat there all afternoon, but he had to come up with a plan that would move Elingale toward independence.

The rebellion against Lord Creedy had been successful, and the days of suffering under his cruel whip were gone forever. But how were the Elwins going to run the day-to-day operation of the island? Who was going to organize the fieldwork and ship the grain? Sure, everything was in place to do this, but no one was in charge to make it happen. His father, Boyne, would have been the appropriate person for the job, but he was dead.

Thand flashed back to the day when his father's fellow workers brought him home. He was still alive but unconscious. Boyne had led a team of three cutters into a field where the deadly spider, Mactabilis, was known to live. Mactabilis wasn't an ordinary spider. It was the size of a large dog, with bristly, gray and tan hair that blended perfectly with the underbrush. The spider had multiple red eyes that looked everywhere at once. Eight legs and claw-like pincers made the spider fast and deadly. Lord Creedy had known the danger but sent the workers anyhow. Halfway through the day the spider attacked. The men had beaten the spider back, but not before he bit Boyne. They brought him home, where he suffered terribly for several days. Then, at the age of fourteen, Thand became the head of the family.

He stood and began to walk along the beach. Talking out loud to himself, he began to formulate a plan: "No one has worked for at least a week, and the fields need tending. As of today, the celebration of Creedy's defeat is over. I need to get everybody back to the jobs they were doing before all this happened. That's the easy part. But once we start harvesting grain again, what are we going to do with it? Who's going to run the grain mill, and who's going to supervise the docks? I need to talk to the grain merchants and ship captains. How do I communicate with people not on the island? Will they listen to an Elwin? We also need three new horses. Where are they going to come from?"

His chest tightened with each new question. There were no answers down here on the beach, so he began to wander back to the village

Up ahead, he saw something bright lying on the sandy trail. Maybe it was just a sunny spot playing tricks on his eyes. But as he got closer, he realized it was a feather. He leaned over and picked up a long white plume. He judged the length to be about three hands long. Slowly, quizzically, he turned it. What bird would possess such a feather?

Maybe it belonged to the white-tailed tropic bird. Thand shook his head; there was no black band near the end of the feather. He thought about the other birds on the island, but none came to mind. This must truly be a rare feather.

Thand combed the area looking for another clue and soon found a ruby red feather. His pulse quickened as he picked it up and compared the two stunning plumes. He began to slowly nod his head. The veins and symmetry were the same on both feathers. Only the shafts were different lengths. *Was it possible?* The hair on his arms stood up as a thrill raced through his body.

"It must be. It has to be…Of course!" he shouted. "It's the Kookachoo Bird's tail feather."

Thand's eyes sparkled as he recalled the ruby-red Kookachoo Bird. The legend of this mythical bird claimed that the person lucky enough to find the long, white tail feather would have good luck and prosperity throughout the remainder of life. This was extraordinary! He let out a yell that caused the birds to flutter away.

The Kookachoo Bird only sheds its feathers once in a hundred years, and I found it. Is this the help I needed to transform Elingale?

He recalled seeing the bird right after the Black Storm in Elingale. He had even exchanged thoughts with the bird. It was like a silent conversation that took place in his mind. He had asked for the feather to help him free Princess Sharman from Creedy's dungeon. The bird had told him he could achieve the job without the feather. But this new task was a far greater challenge. Many people's lives depended on his success. It must have known that he would need the power of the feather in order to accomplish his goal.

With the feather, he could transform Elingale into a real paradise. Plenty of food. Bigger houses. No one would want for anything. After all the hardships they had suffered under Creedy's rule and Baylock's spells, it was time Elingale had some good fortune. He waved the feather above his head in a figure eight and hooted once more. It would be his honor to make it happen.

Thand felt lighthearted, like his burden had been lifted. The feather would solve all of his problems. He started back toward home whistling a tune.

It only took a few steps before Thand's whistle dried up. He looked toward the sky and heard the silent words of the Great Wizard Enunciation: "Beware. Power corrupts."

He ran a hand through his silky hair. *Am I strong enough to do this?*

He walked a few steps, and then stopped again. *How do I make this work? Do I need some magic words? Maybe I just make a wish and it comes true.*

He closed his eyes, held out his palm, and wished for some coins to appear. When he opened his eyes, his palm was empty.

Darn, I knew it wouldn't be that easy.

His brow wrinkled as he wondered how the villagers would react once they knew he had the magical feather. They would be delighted of course, but their expectations would change immediately. They would assume that he could solve all problems and heal all ailments, or wave the feather in the air and instantly fulfill their wishes.

That's okay, but how?

He began to chew on his bottom lip. *What if I can't do the things that the feather promises? Will the villagers think I'm being deceitful, holding back the power so that I can keep it all for myself? Will they call me Lord Greedy?*

Thand turned toward the sea and wished he could wave a magic wand and bring the princess back. She would know what to do.

Surely the Kookachoo Bird wouldn't have left it for him unless he was meant to use it. If he could communicate with the bird again, maybe...

He closed his eyes and imagined the ruby-red bird, with its ivory white beak, streaking across the sky, its white tail feather trailing like a wisp of smoke. The distinctive sound, *Koo-kook-a-choo, Koo-kook-a-choo*, echoed in his head. But quickly the melodic call changed to, *How, how? How does the feather work?*

He opened his eyes and looked around the forest, hoping to see the Kookachoo Bird, but it was not in sight.

Maybe I'm not smart enough to use the feather. After all, I only learned to read recently.

Then another thought occurred to him. *Carrying a twenty-inch feather into the village will attract too much attention. It might be a better idea to hide it until I understand how to control the power.*

Looking left, he saw a deer track. The forest would be a perfect hideaway. It held so many secrets—one more wouldn't matter.

He recalled a large oak tree where he liked to sit and think. In that tree, about thirty feet up the craggy trunk, there was a cavity that looked like an open mouth. Above that opening, there were two big knots that resembled a pair of closed eyes. His brother Eschon had named it Facetree a long time ago, and the name had stuck.

Dodging thorn bushes and low hanging branches, he ran down the narrow trail until the distinctive landmark overshadowed him. He stared up at the tree. The outspread branches and face combined to look like a huge sentry guarding the forest, protecting everyone beneath its canopy. Without a second thought, he climbed skyward.

Standing on a shoulder branch, he cautiously reached into the mouth-like opening to make sure it was dry and free of woodland critters. Next, he opened his shirt and removed the feather.

His brow drew tight with worry. *Is this right? Maybe Eschon knows how it works.* He shrugged. *Eschon only knows the legend.*

Wanting to safeguard the feather further, he summoned the elemental gods and asked the tree to protect his feather. Then, before he could change his mind, he placed it inside the cavity and descended toward the forest floor.

He emerged from the forest at the top of the hill overlooking the village. Some children were playing and ran toward him, calling his name. The sight lifted his uncertain mood, and a bright smile replaced his wrinkled brow. He knelt down, gathered the children around him, and then clapped. "Who can read?"

All the hands shot into the air.

"Good, that means you're smart enough to solve my riddle," he said as he looked each one in the eye.

"What belongs to you, but others use it more than you do?"

The kids tilted their heads in a quizzical look. They looked at each other but no one spoke.

"Give up?" he said with a playful look on his face.

They all nodded rapidly.

"It's your name."

The children looked confused for a second and then burst out laughing.

"Now, you lads make your own riddle. And when you're finished, come see me."

The kids took off down the hill and toward the village. The boys raced ahead, trying to be first, while the girls flapped their hands and laughed at the silly competition.

Thand watched the children for a moment, and then looked across the valley. Low stone walls crisscrossed the rolling hills that penned in bleating sheep. The forest to the north and the bald mountain off in the distance looked the same as always. Even the large stone manor house that had once belonged to the corrupt landlord, Lord Creedy, was sitting unchanged.

When he reached home, his mother was in her garden tending to her flowers. He gave her a quick peck on the cheek and then walked over and opened the arched cottage door.

He walked to his room and flopped on the bed. The burden of responsibility had returned. *Now what? I have a magical feather that I don't know how to use and no plan to move Elingale forward.*

"Eschon, come in here. I need to talk to you."

Eschon walked through the bedroom door telling a joke. "Hey, Thand, have you heard the one about the witch, the warlock, and the magician?"

"Eschon, I have no time for jokes. Here, sit beside me. I have something important to tell you."

Eschon sat. "I'm not going to like this."

"I have good news and bad." Then Thand pulled out the note from Creedy. "Read this."

Eschon read the note and frowned. "I don't like this. Who gave it to you?"

"Someone must have come in through the window and left it on my bed."

"It's a warning, but we sort of knew this already. It's probably Creedy's way of giving us a parting shot."

"I agree. Still, we need to be aware. That's the bad news."

Thand blew out a long, slow breath as he thought about what to say. "All right, I'm going to tell you something extraordinary, but you must keep it a secret. Promise?"

Eschon spit in his palm. Thand did the same, and both shook hands. The secret was safe.

"Okay. This afternoon I took a walk down to the beach, but when I started back home, I found a white feather lying on the trail."

"So what?" Eschon shrugged.

Thand stood quickly. "So what!? Do you remember the legend of the Kookachoo Bird and the power that is given to the person who finds its feather? That's what I'm talking about."

"What? Are you sure it's the right feather?"

Thand nodded yes. "If you saw it, you'd have no doubt."

Eschon hooted, ran around the room, and in his enthusiasm knocked over a chair. Embarrassed by his overreaction, he cleared his throat and said, "That's great."

"Be quiet!" Thand chided. "We don't want anyone else to know about this."

"It doesn't matter. We're going to be rich, like Lord Creedy."

"That's not what I'm thinking, Eschon. If the power of the feather is true, I want to use it for good, not evil."

"You can do that and we'll still be rich."

"I'm not sure how people will react to me once they know I have the feather. They'll probably think that I have the power to change their lives, to make them wealthy, and to heal their ailments."

"Well, kin, you will have the power to do that. Has anything happened yet?"

"So far, nothing has changed. And since I didn't know how people would react, I hid it in a tree."

"A tree? Something that important is in a tree?"

"It's safe. I'll go back for it when I'm ready."

Eschon crossed his arms and began tapping his foot excitedly. "Now, kin, not later. I want to see it and feel the power."

Thand was already twitching to hold the feather again. He looked out the window and then slapped his knee. "Okay. Let's go."

Chapter 10

THE JUNGLE CANOPY was dense, and like the lid on a kettle, it trapped the oppressive moisture in the rain forest. Cayman was raised in this type of climate and wasn't bothered. He sat on a stool, rubbing a pumice stone across his blade. When he looked up, the visitors emerged from the jungle. The princess' blouse clung to her like a second skin, while perspiration rolled down Oden's forehead. Adding to their suffering, a swarm of biting flies had descended on them.

Cayman quietly chuckled at their misery and waited for them to come over. He turned on his charm again: "I hope de villagers were helpful."

The princess fanned at the flies. "They didn't know anything about my uncle, but we did get a warning about Skull Island. What do you know about that awful-sounding place?"

Cayman raised his eyes, sensing an opportunity. "Meh know a lot about dat island and many more. Yuh could use a person like me to help find yuh uncle and keep yuh safe."

"Take you with us?" Oden said as he realized the insinuation. "Not going to happen."

Princess Sharman gave Oden an annoyed glance. "Why wouldn't we want to use every means possible to find my uncle?

If Cayman is familiar with the area, why not? It makes sense to have somebody like him on board."

Now Oden looked annoyed. "We don't know anything about this man. He's probably a pirate. And believe me, you can't trust them."

"Reformed pirate," Cayman said with emphasis. "I'm through with piracy. I have seen too much fighting and killing. Besides, de pay is lousy. Ah captain takes most of de booty and leaves little for de hardworking men."

Oden snorted. "You mean you were thrown off your marauding ship."

"Let's leave it at I'm retired, but I have ah wealth of knowledge dat I'm willing to share."

Princess Sharman frowned and gave Cayman a questioning look. "You aren't one of the pirates that attacked *Odyssey*, are you?"

"Nuh," said Cayman, "but I'd heard de story. *Odyssey* was loaded with treasure, and de buccaneers were eager to get on board and take it. But de ship was not supposed to be set on fire. A few prisoners were taken and sold in de slave market, but everything else was destroyed in the fire."

Sharman's eyes widened. "What do you mean by taken to the slave market?"

"Selling people is very profitable. Ah dignitary like your uncle would've fetched ah mighty good price. And yuh would be worth ah treasure chest full of gems to some rich man looking for ah beauty."

"What? You can't sell me! That's ridiculous! I am a free woman, a princess!"

"Not to ah pirate. You're just ah commodity, something of value."

The princess' face paled as she wrapped her arms around herself.

"Yes," Cayman agreed. "I hate slavery. It's the reason dat I took a walk. During our last adventure we took ah ship, but dere was two children on board. I suddenly understood dat if something happens to those children, it's my fault. I begged the captain to let them go, but he took them anyway. At de next port, I walked away."

Oden scoffed. "What a farce. You, an honorable pirate?"

Cayman ground his teeth; the muscle cords on his neck tightened. He turned toward the princess.

"I was forcefully taken from my parents at the age of ten and made to work as ah cabin boy. Over time I learned de ways of sailors and learned de way of pirates. When you live with buccaneers yuh take on their ways. But after years of seein' so much suffering, I changed my mind and decided to retire."

Oden sneered. "Must've been recent."

Cayman turned to the princess. "I'd be happy to tell yuh the story. Then yuh might—"

"Enough of the sad tale," Oden cut in. "It's time we get back—without him!"

The princess sighed. "Look, Oden, this is a decision that the captain will make, not you."

Once on board, the three of them proceeded toward the captain's cabin. Oden's lips were pinched tight as he took long angry strides across the deck. Princess Sharman tried desperately to match his pace, finally running the last few yards to the cabin door. Cayman followed at a short distance while mentally preparing to convince the captain that he was indispensable. He ignored the distrustful stares of the other sailors.

Once inside the cabin, Princess Sharman stepped in front of Oden and explained why she had brought Cayman aboard. "He's familiar with the nearby islands and would be valuable in the search for my uncle."

Oden waited for the princess to finish her pitch, and then he stepped up. His eyes narrowed. "Don't trust him."

Captain Boreas stuck his hands in his pocket and studied Cayman for a moment. "Well I've heard these two. What do you have to say for yourself?"

Cayman knew this was not the time to be arrogant, but yet he needed to show he was confident. Using his best English, he said, "Captain, sir. I have vast knowledge of these waters and the surrounding islands. I know the currents and how they can affect someone adrift. I can identify most pirate ships at first glance, and I have been sailing since I was ten years old. I need no training."

The captain rubbed his jaw for a moment and then, in a flat-toned voice, spoke. "Given the limited amount of time we have, anyone who can help speed up the search will be welcomed. You'll be released when we get to Empeerean."

Oden began to speak, but the captain raised his hand and then looked hard into Cayman's eyes. "But if I see anything that makes me believe yar not telling us the truth, I'll treat ya like a pirate and have ya tossed into the sea with yar hands tied behind yar back. Ya understand?"

"Yes, sir." Cayman saluted.

Chapter 11

THE WIND SPEED was perfect. The wave heights were minimal. And judging by the clouds, a storm wasn't likely. Unfortunately, Baylock's damaged boat wouldn't be able to take advantage of the ideal conditions. The bump on his head still throbbed, but the bleeding had stopped. He had found an old scarf and then wrapped it tightly around his ankle to make walking a little less painful. Above, a few squawking birds circled around, as if taunting his slow speed. He snarled and threw a stone at the gulls.

The trip to his new home would take forever at this speed, but Baylock's tedious travel gave him time to think about his new plan for greatness. It would be far more ambitious than his last spell. He would use the lessons from his hated father, Arawn.

The old man had taught him that words were the most powerful force on earth. They could be put to good use, as in words of encouragement, or to destructive use through malicious comments. When Baylock was a child, Arawn had chosen to punish with words. He'd use terms such as simpleton and dimwit to make his son feel stupid. And phrases like "You're a failure and I'm ashamed to call you my son." These words cut out his heart and left behind nothing but hatred. The pain of a lash fades quickly, but the pain of vicious words stays forever.

Rulers had risen and fallen by the words they chose. If Baylock had the power to control words, then he would decide the winners and losers of the world. His brilliant new plan would create an incantation that could make this possible. He would decide what was spoken, and the rest would be magically censored. No magician on earth would be powerful enough to stop him because he could control the words of any wizard's incantation. Emperors and kings, czars and sultans would bow to him.

At last, a massive, skull-shaped stone came rising out of the sea. The bizarre rock sat at the tip of an uninhabited island that made the perfect location for a fortress.

Three years ago, he'd met a man who shaped stone by drilling holes and packing them with gunpowder. He'd hired the stone sculptor to fashion the rock into the contour of a skull. The man was a destructive genius. Blowing up rocks to make a work of art seemed like an impossible task. Then, after the demolition was finished, various craftsmen were brought in to finish the job.

Baylock didn't want a fortress with high walls and turrets. That would attract too much attention. But a stronghold, shaped like a human skull, would be synonymous with danger and death. Anyone coming near the island would naturally assume the place was evil. And they would be correct. A few human skeletons bore witness to that fact.

Baylock let a smile creep over his face. Cannon shots could pound it all day and barely produce a scratch. His creation was a masterpiece. The outside looked like it had been shaped over the centuries by the sea and wind, but below the rock surface was an opulent home he called the Cranium. Too bad the workers had died so soon after its completion.

Baylock skillfully sailed his boat through the serpentine channel of the coral reef and into the mouth of the cave. Once inside, the channel split in two. The shorter canal ended at a small pier located in front of the Cranium. The second channel continued deep into the cave and then disappeared into a narrow gap behind a wall of granite. There was a large opening beyond this wall where his bohes now lived. They had chased the small bats from their roost with their fiery breath and then claimed it for themselves.

The wizard tied up the boat and hobbled into Cranium. The great hall was thirty feet from the floor to the dome ceiling and at least fifty feet wide. A grand, double-sided staircase curved up from separate sides of the room and met in the middle to form a single staircase.

Baylock began to ascend the left-hand side of the marble staircase, oblivious to the grandeur of the great hall. His thoughts were still on the Elwins and the indignation of being chased from Lapis Lazuli.

He stopped at the landing and looked across the great hall. There was no claustrophobic feeling in here; the six walls and domed ceiling were decorated with porcelain tiles that were created to look like the surrounding sea. The mural was so accurate that the stone walls seemed to be made of glass.

He turned around and ascended to a midlevel balcony where his sleeping quarters were located. From this level, another set of stairs led up to a third level where his library and laboratory were located. He walked along the balcony and began climbing the next set of stairs. His thoughts turned from the Elwins and back to his master plan.

Words. So simple a concept, yet so brilliant an idea.

He looked at his panting dog, Caedo. "Once I've created this new spell, my furry friend, no one will be able to speak out against me. No one will be able to countermand my edicts. I'll have the power to conquer nations."

Baylock's adrenaline was pumping. Arriving on the landing out of breath, he paused for a moment and looked at the remarkable tiled mural. It was so masterful that the seabirds seemed to be flying.

The wizard entered a room where a large, triangular window looked out to the sea. The window had been coated in half silver—so that he could see out, but no one could see inside. He reached for his manual of magic, anxious to begin the search.

Chapter 12

CAYMAN WALKED TOWARD the front of the boat to begin his first assignment. His thoughts were on the princess. If not for her, he would probably be swatting mosquitoes and drinking rum with outlaws. He needed a new start and she had given him one.

His first assignment was to braid some frayed rope that the rats had chewed. It was a very low-level job that was usually performed by a junior member of the crew. He got it and was not angry. This menial assignment was to show the rest of the crew that the new guy was getting no special treatment. Besides, it gave him something to do as they sailed toward Skull Island.

As he sat on a barrel, twisting loose strands of hemp back into the rope, the wind brought the sound of talking sailors. His ears perked up when he heard his name. One sailor, whose voice sounded gravelly, said that Cayman had pulled his sword on Oden and was lucky that the first mate hadn't cut him to pieces. Another voice claimed that Cayman had tried to poison the princess.

An officer came up from below deck, saw the men loafing, and told them to move on or he'd flog someone. The men jumped up and began to scatter, but Cayman heard Scarface say, "He's bad luck, I tell ya. I seen a rat scurry off de ship when he came on. Dem rodents know when there's trouble on board."

Cayman shrugged the words off. He didn't care about the crew's attitude. It wouldn't be long before he moved on. He was on a quest to find a former shipmate and even a score. Moving from ship to ship was the quickest way to find him.

He finished repairing the ropes and stood. Steering clear of as many people as possible, he moved around, studying the ship. Sails, pulleys, and ropes were all in excellent condition. The deck was clean and free of loose cargo. The sailors wore clean uniforms with no tears. All were telling signs of a strong captain and good crew.

It was near sunset when the crow's nest called, "Land ho. Dead ahead." A skull-like rock rose out of the ocean and appeared to be waiting for them to come closer. Cayman frowned; it was the worst time of day to see Skull Island for the first time.

In the crow's nest, the watchman called out the change in the ship's position: "Look ahead, starboard." Then he added in a softer voice, "And pray to Neptune."

Like a blood-drenched head, the cave on Skull Island shimmered in the crimson light. The descending sun had transformed the orange-colored sea to butchery red and cast deep shadows across the island. Glowing red rays reflected off the glass window surfaces, reminiscent of the devil's fiery eyes. To the superstitious seamen, the open mouth of the cave appeared to be the grand entrance into hell.

Sensing trouble, Captain Boreas stepped out of his cabin. The deck and sails were dyed in the red of the sunset. He looked forward and frowned at the sight. Then Oden appeared on his right side. He glanced at the first mate and then said in a calm voice,

"Drop anchor. The crew seems unsettled. This is close enough for tonight."

Cayman assumed that Princess Sharman had been frightened by this evenings' spectacle. A visit to reassure her that it was only the setting sun that had produced the ghoulish illusion would be a nice gesture. As justification for his visit, he grabbed a biscuit and a plate of salted fish from the galley and then climbed up the companionway. She was the closest thing he had to a friend, and though his action might be perceived as bold, he thought she would understand it was just a friendly visit.

He knocked on the door. A muted voice asked, "Who's there?"

"It's me, the notorious pirate Cayman, come to bring yuh some vittles."

The door opened halfway. His eyes grew large as he looked at the princess. She was wearing a silver silk shirt and black leather pants. Her hair hung loose across her shoulders. In her haste to answer the knock, she had only fastened the top button on her blouse. Her thin, oval face and muted green eyes were instantly burned into his memory.

Sweeping her long, auburn hair back, she gave him an inviting smile.

"What can I do for you, Cayman?"

"I brought a plate of food," he said as he handed her the platter. "I thought yuh might be hungry. Can I come in?"

"Aren't you brash? Coming here uninvited and asking to come in. You could ruin my reputation."

"Just trying to be friendly, dat's all. What do yuh mean by brash?"

The princess took the tray and put it on the table. She then went over to a shelf, picked up her dictionary, and went back to the doorway.

"Look it up."

Cayman looked at the book like it was a poisonous snake and refused to take it.

Sharman gave an understanding nod and then, in a kind voice, said, "I see. You're not a reader. That's okay. It's not a disgrace if you can't, but it's a tragedy if you don't try to learn."

Cayman looked at his feet. "I can read…a little. When I was a cabin boy, de ship's cook knew how to read and taught me a few words. But de captain said it was a waste of time: 'You need to learn how to swing a sword, not read a book.' After dat I never bothered."

"I'm sorry to hear that. Reading and writing can be much more useful than a sword. Tell me, what is more powerful: a shiny sword to fight a war or some simple words to stop one?"

"I've never thought about it like dat." He raised his head as an idea came to him. "Yuh read. Can yuh teach me?"

"I can help you with a few of the basics now. But first, you must assure me that you'll continue after tonight. I have a saying: 'Learning to read is the key to success.' Remember it and it will serve you well."

He nodded a reluctant yes. The princess took a step back from the door and cautiously studied him. He noticed that her eyes lingered on the jagged pink scar on his left leg. A phantom pain shot down his leg as a reminder of how he'd acquired the scar.

She went to touch it but then pulled back. In a gentle voice she said, "Tell me about the scar on your leg. I didn't notice it before. Is it painful? There must be a story."

A deep, throaty laughed followed. "Yes, there's a story. But I'd rather not tell it standing out here."

She looked over his shoulder, and then tapped one finger on her lip. "I guess it's all right. Come in, but don't close the door."

Cayman's smile wavered. Her guarded answer wasn't a rejection, but it wasn't an unrestricted invitation either. He crossed his arms and leaned a shoulder against the doorframe, deciding to play it safe.

"Where I come from, in de southern hemisphere, we have a ritual dat all boys must undergo in order to be considered an adult. When a boy is ready to prove his masculinity, usually around the age of twelve or thirteen, he is taken to a place on the river dat is known to be infested with man-eating piranha fish. In order to show his courage, he must swim the river to the far shore."

The princess' eyes widened, doubting the story.

"Once yuh dive into the river, yuh must continue swimming, no matter what, until yuh reach de other shore. If yuh're courageous, yuh'll ignore the pain of de piranha bites and make it to the other side. If yuh are fearful, or hesitate at any point, de fish will pull yuh down and eat yuh alive."

The princess tapped her fingers together. "I don't believe that. You're joking!"

Cayman scowled and pointed to several small scars on his right leg. "Du yuh doubt me now?"

"I guess not. If you say it's true, then I'll believe you. But that's a bizarre custom. Are many boys lost during the ritual?"

"Only de weak."

"So that jagged scar is from the piranhas?"

"No, but I got it at de same time." He looked down again at his leg and touched the scar lightly. "I was so focused on getting across de river, dat I didn't see de caiman lurking in de reeds. A caiman is what you'd call an alligator.

"I was splashing and fumbling from exhaustion by de time I reached de shallow water. De caiman must have mistaken me for a wounded animal. Because he jumped out and locked his jaw on my leg, then began pulling me back into de river. Luckily, I had my dagger with me, and I was able to kill him. De village was so impressed dat I survived de two dangers dey gave me a new name, Cayman Azrail. De name sort of means dat I'm de angel of death for de caimans."

"Well, Cayman Azrail, come in and I'll give you your first reading lesson. And we'll work on getting rid of the *de* and *dat* in your speech."

Cayman was pleased by her response and stepped across the threshold into her room. Suddenly, he felt an iron grip on his shoulder. Oden yanked him backward into the hallway.

"This deck is off-limits for all sailors," Oden yelled unkindly. "If I see you here again, you'll be thrown into the brig."

Blood rushed to Cayman's head and he curled his hands into a fist. He stepped up to Oden's face, baring his teeth.

"Go ahead; I'd love to have an excuse."

"No," shouted the princess. "Stop. Please don't fight."

Cayman thought about the consequences, took a deep breath, and then cleared his throat.

"Yes, sir!" he said in a sneering manner. Then he turned and deliberately bumped Oden as he pushed past.

Before Oden could retaliate, Princess Sharman grabbed him by the back of his shirt and yanked him into the room, slamming the door on Cayman.

Cayman heard a thump, then a crash, as if someone had fallen. *If he hurts her, I kill him.* He reached for the doorknob but stopped.

"Get up!" he heard the princess say. "What's that about?" Who made you my bodyguard? I'm capable of taking care of myself."

Then he heard Oden's muted voice. "But I thought—"

"Cayman's no threat. He's just trying to be friendly."

"Friendly?" Oden's voice was stronger. "Didn't you see that look in his eyes? He has more than friendly on his mind."

"What are you talking about, Oden? I've never seen you act like this before, and I can tell you that I don't appreciate it. Now, get out of my cabin and leave me alone."

Cayman dashed behind a support column as Oden came tearing out of the room and up the gangway. *Why had Oden reacted like that? Princess Sharman had it right. I was only being friendly.*

Walking in the opposite direction toward the galley he thought, *Wasn't I?*

Chapter 13

THAND ARRIVED AT Facetree, winded from the run. His brother had won the race and was already climbing the tree.

"Hey, slow down. I should go first," Thand wheezed.

"Don't worry. I know where to look. Remember, I'm the one who named it."

Thand protested again. He wasn't sure if he wanted Eschon to touch the feather, but it was too late to stop him. His brother was already fifteen feet above him.

Eschon got to the opening and steadied himself on the tree branch before reaching into the hole. He groped around in search of the downy softness.

"Are you sure this is the right tree? There's nothing in here but a bunch of leaves."

Thand chuckled. "You're an annoying little brother."

"I'm serious. There's no feather here, just a bunch of dried leaves."

The air left Thand's lungs as if he had just been punched. For a moment he seemed paralyzed. Then, swallowing hard, he reached for the next branch and resumed climbing. Moments later, he was standing on the limb with Eschon, sweating profusely. Thand shoved his brother aside and then glanced inside the cavity. Nothing. He didn't trust his eyes and began pulling out everything he touched.

This can't be happening, he thought. His hands began to shake as he continued to toss leaves out of the opening.

"It's not here! I can't believe this. Who would've taken it? That feather is mine. They have no right to it."

"Calm down, kin. Maybe the wind got hold of it. Let's search the ground."

The late afternoon sun was already low in the sky, and the dimming light was made weaker by the numerous leaves.

They began at the base of Facetree, kicking leaves and branches, and then worked outward. When their initial search produced no results, they got down on their hands and knees. Despite the poor light, the two boys continued to comb through the forest floor until it was nearly impossible to see.

"Nothing!" Thand yelled, slamming his fist into the ground. He rolled onto his back and looked up at the tree, replaying the moment when he'd placed the feather into the cavity. He was positive that this was the right tree; after all, how many trees looked like they had a face? He remembered speaking to the tree and it had acknowledged him.

"Some guardian you are," he mumbled.

Eschon reached down to help him stand. "There's a new moon tonight. The woods will be as dark as pitch. First thing in the morning, we'll come back."

Thand refused his hand.

Eschon tried again. "You can't spend the night in the forest alone. You know wolves hunt at night?"

Thand looked up at Facetree. "I'm not leaving until I have that feather in my hand."

Eschon shrugged. "Have it your way. I'm going home to eat."

When Eschon returned to Facetree Thand was sitting with his back on the tree and chin touching his chest. Eschon kicked his foot and called out Thand's name.

He opened his eyes slowly and looked around. The light was weak from the early hour. Confused, he patted the ground and then looked up and met Eschon's stare.

"I guess you're right. I must be possessed. I dreamt the feather was calling my name."

"Mother was asking for you this morning. I told her you must have left early."

Thand stretched his neck and rolled his shoulder. Clasping his knees tightly to his chest, he rocked. "I'm afraid I'll never know the power of the feather."

"If someone else discovered it, you'll know."

Thand rolled onto his back and closed his eyes. "Don't say that. It's a terrible thought."

Eschon smiled. "Imagine the power of the words he could write if he turned the Kookachoo feather into a pen."

He walked over and sat alongside his brother. "What if someone else did find the feather? Couldn't you just take it from him?"

"It's not that simple," Thand said with a heavy sigh. "The legend says the power is lost if it is stolen or not given freely. Grabbing the feather away from someone wouldn't work. If someone picked up my feather yesterday, then it's theirs, and there's nothing I can do about it. Maybe if I could talk him into giving it up voluntarily, then the force would return to me. But no one I know would turn over that much power without a fight."

The morning's sunrays were just beginning to penetrate the leafy canopy. A hammering woodpecker made Thand look up. The sunlight was illuminating something silvery in the tree. His mouth went dry. He jumped to his feet and pointed to the top of a nearby tree, and then, without explaining, began climbing.

Something white was hanging from the edge of a squirrel's nest. He climbed toward the leaf-and-twig framework that formed the squirrel's home. A few feet below the nest, he could see a large black squirrel staring straight down at him, blocking his path. Its feet were set wide apart and its dark tail swished side to side. The animal appeared ready to defend its nest.

Thand swatted his hand. The squirrel scurried up the tree several branches and then turned, ready to pounce if anyone came closer.

"Don't worry, Mr. Squirrel. I'm not going to wreck your house. I just want to remove one piece."

Thand pulled on the white feather and then again. Suddenly, it came loose. He was light-headed from the joy. "I found it! It's the Kookachoo Bird's feather. I found it."

The shouting frightened the squirrel. Its tail bristled as it screeched loudly, and then it pounced on Thand's hand, scratching and biting. The surprise and pain caused his hand to spring open, losing his grip on the branch. He tumbled through the tree, bouncing off of several limbs as he went down. The ground raced up and hit him with a heavy thud.

Eschon ran to his brother's aid. Thand's eyes were glassy but he was awake. He clutched his right side while holding the feather up for his brother to see. But when Eschon reached for it, he swiftly pulled his hand back.

"No," he said in an unworldly voice. "No one can touch it but me."

The sudden movement of his arm sent a wave of pain down his side. "Aww, I think I hurt my ribs."

"Good, maybe the pain will shock some sense into you. Your obsession with that feather is beginning to twist your thinking."

"You're just jealous that I found it and not you."

Eschon's eyes narrowed. "What? Why are you acting like this?"

"Just leave! I'll take care of myself."

"Thand that was a long fall. Put the feather down and let me look at your side."

"So you can grab it and run? No way. Just leave alone. Go home."

Eschon opened his mouth to challenge that statement, but stopped short. "Good idea."

Chapter 14

CAYMAN STEPPED ON deck. Expecting the fresh smell of the sea, he breathed in deeply. Instead, the morning air was tinted with the smell of death. Cayman's nose wrinkled. *Skull Island.*

He looked up to the quarterdeck and saw the first mate, Oden. He still hadn't sorted out his own feelings from last night, but for the sake of the princess, he would try to forget the incident with Oden.

Morning inspection was about to begin. He hustled to the center of the ship where the sailors where lining up in neat rows. They stood stoically with their feet spread apart and hands clasped neatly behind their backs.

Cayman laughed to himself. He couldn't imagine getting a pirate crew to line up this precise. A door slammed, a seagull squawked, and the serenity of the moment was shattered. He lined up with the other men and snapped to attention—chin up, chest out, eyes front.

Captain Boreas, stern-faced, a hitch in his step, strode across the deck. Cayman watched out of the corner of his eyes while the captain walked down the line inspecting the front row of sailors.

"It's my understanding," he barked, "that several of you have questioned the wisdom of exploring this island. And a few of you are unhappy with our new crew member."

Cayman cringed. He wanted to fit in, not stand out.

"This is my ship, and I decide where we go and who sails on it. Is that understood? If you don't like it, I still have room in the brig next to the scoundrel, Creedy. Or you can swim to the next island."

All sailors' eyes stayed fixed in place, staring at nothing it seemed. Boreas looked up. The flag was flapping strong. "Looks like a good day for sailing, the captain said. Then he turned and nodded toward Oden, who snapped to attention and barked, "Dismissed."

The sailors broke formation. A dozen clambered up the rigging and onto the yardarms, while others hurried toward the bow. Cayman had not been assigned any specific duties yet, so he joined the men on the capstan and walked in a circle, raising the anchor from the seafloor. In a show of unity, he joined with the men in singing a sea shanty:

> *"Seven long years I courted Sally,*
> *But I didn't care for her dillydally.*
> *So I signed on board the Trident Seas,*
> *An' when I come home she had left me.*
> *Yo-ho, Yo-ho, she must've turned madly."*

The strong wind helped propel the ship forward, and they reached top speed quickly. At this pace, they should be on the island very soon.

Cayman was walking from the bow, his duty done, when he saw the princess at the side rail looking pale. He knew the signs of seasickness and walked over.

"Look out to the horizon. It's a straight line. Focus on that and ignore the waves. You'll feel better shortly."

The princess was trying to follow his instructions when the sails inexplicably went slack. The ship began to lose speed and stopped. Then it appeared as if the ship was moving backwards, away from the island. An unseen current was carrying them away.

Cayman was puzzled at first, but then remembered where they were.

The other sailors stopped working and turned toward the captain, hoping for an answer. Murmurs began amongst the crew. Boreas yelled, "Get back to work," then tilted his head and motioned Oden toward his cabin.

"What's happening?" asked Sharman.

"Don't worry," Cayman said as he left the princess at the side rail.

He hurried past the confused sailors and went to the captain's cabin. After a moment of hesitation, he raised his hand and knocked on the door.

"What is this, a town hall meeting?" growled the captain through the door.

Cayman opened the door and stepped in. Oden and the captain were studying the charts.

"What do you want?" the captain snapped. "Do you know anything about this?"

"Sir, I think I can explain dis."

Oden sighed heavily, "Yes, the man with all of the answers."

Cayman shrugged off the comment and remembered to use his best English. "This isn't the first time that slack wind and reverse currents have occurred in this area. Some captains believe that there is a magical aura encircling Skull Island—like an invisible dome protecting the cave from intruders."

Boreas ran a hand over his bald head. "Magic dome? That's hard to believe. But something strange is happening. I can feel it in my leg."

Oden turned to the captain. "Everything we've heard about

this place is strange. It could be some magical device generating a strong undercurrent."

Cayman spoke up. "Maybe, but that doesn't account for the lack of wind."

Oden nodded and conceded the point grudgingly.

"I've sailed these waters in the past," Cayman said, looking at the captain. "I might have a way to swim the tide."

The lack of an objection was his sign to continue.

"In the summer months, like now, it's common to have powerful afternoon thunderstorms. Instead of avoiding de storm, we could utilize that strength. De heavy winds generated might give us enough speed to break through the barrier and push onto the island."

Oden looked at the captain and shook his head negatively. "His plan means we have to sit until the weather changes. If the thunderstorm doesn't appear, we'll have wasted a full day. I was told that we have no time for that."

Captain Boreas spoke up. "If you're right, Cayman, we could be on that island before dinner. Or if you're wrong, we could be splintered into a thousand pieces."

The captain glanced at Oden. "It's a day's sail to the next island, so either way, we've lost time. I don't like running from a problem. I'll risk it."

Chapter 15

BAYLOCK CLIMBED THE steps to the third level of the Cranium and entered the library. The vaulted room occupied half of the space on the top level. A single window, shaped to look like a skull's eye socket, provided light. While this room was much smaller than his last library, he still managed to pack in over a thousand textbooks, manuals, and essays.

For several days he had combed through his books searching for an idea, a concept, or a theory that would give him the ability to manipulate speech.

Just before midnight, he'd come upon a tome titled *Gray Matter: Science of the Brain*. It was a thick book with many illustrations. He read through the pages and discovered that a section of the brain, called the temporal lobe, was responsible for controlling speech. His heart rate increased as he read on, absorbing every word. When the chapter ended, he closed the book, leaned back in his chair, and mused. *A spell to manipulate that part of the brain would give me absolute control over speech.*

His adrenaline began to surge. His sleepy eyes became bright. With a head full of fresh ideas, he raced down the hall to the laboratory. The room was filled with herbs: lemon balm, rosemary, and lavender. Colorful Camu, buckthorn, and maqui berry sprigs hung from the ceiling, waiting to be ground into powder. A distilling flask bubbled on a bench below the window. His eyes lit up. *The possibilities.*

"Hmmm," he muttered mindlessly while pinching the skin on his throat. For a conjuration of this magnitude, he would need to include all the natural elements: earth, water, fire, and air. He inspected the inventory in the magically sealed cabinet that contained the rarest of elements.

The first component required was soil from the Garden of Creation. This was a very precious and potent element, and replenishing it would nearly be impossible. But over the years he used the ingredient sparingly and still had a half-filled jar.

The element water would have to come from the Pond of Life; again, he had only used it for his most powerful spells and still had several vials hidden away. Third was fire, and fire was his specialty. That component would not be a problem.

The last element would be air. He knew how to create wind, but a simple blast would not be enough for a spell of this enormity. Wind like he had created for the Black Storm at Elingale was needed, but its power would have to be a hundred times stronger.

After several hours of experimentation, Baylock's adrenaline began to wear off. The candles had burned low and his back throbbed. He opened his grimoire to look for an incantation, but the words were fuzzy. Rubbing his eyes, he marked the page with a feather and closed the magic book. Sunrise was only a few hours away.

The next morning came fast, but Baylock didn't care. He jumped out of bed and went to the laboratory, forgetting to eat. Fresh ideas floated in and out his head as he tried different combinations. He was sure that the words to the incantation were right, but nothing he did would produce enough wind to carry his words for hundreds of miles. If he was going to take over a kingdom, he needed his words to speed through the city and continue out into the heartland until the entire island had heard the spell.

By late evening he had produced nothing reliable. Worse, his scarce elements were running low.

He scrubbed his hands over his face, lowered his head, and walked to the library. A table near the arch-shaped window contained a decanter of sherry and a book called *Myths and Legends*. He had seen enough books on science to last a lifetime. Maybe some folktales would stimulate fresh thought? After pouring himself a glass of the sweet red wine, he collapsed into his overstuffed chair. He picked up the book and began flipping pages until a drawing of a beautiful bird with outstanding feathers caught his attention. In the world of magic, feathers represented the element air. After a few moments of reading, a smile appeared upon his tired face. This bird, called the Kookachoo Bird, had a magical tail feather that, if it was as powerful as the legend described, would be the perfect element to energize his spell.

He swirled the wine in his glass and pondered. Legends were unverifiable stories handed down from earlier times. As a practical man, he had found most fables to be the equivalent of a good bedtime story. But at this point, all of his scientific ideas had been exhausted. He pondered. *Some people think that magic is just sleight of hand, but they are dead wrong. Maybe there is some truth in these fables.* He read on.

"If true, the Kookachoo Bird's tail feather is exactly what I'm seeking," he said to his trusted old dog, Caedo. "Dynamic and extremely rare. The power has to be awesome. I must get hold of it."

But the story gave no hint as to where the bird resided. He frowned; this was a sign that the legend was probably false. However, there were always exceptions, he reminded himself, as in the folktale of burning rocks. That fable turned out to be true and led to the discovery of sulfur.

He pressed his fingers to his lips, and then nodded curtly. Tomorrow he would begin the search for the Kookachoo Bird.

Chapter 16

THE FAMILY HAD just finished breakfast, and as usual, Thand retired to his bedroom. Outside, the morning sun was shining bright; the air was dry and crisp. A busy humming bird flitted from flower to flower sipping the sweet nectar of Grace's plants.

Thand was trying to write a letter to Princess Sharman when the bedroom door flew open. Eschon stepped in, sat on the side of the bed, and began talking about the dragon bone.

"It's hard to imagine that a dragon was here in our village. I wonder how many years have passed since it died?"

"I'm not really interested, Eschon. Why don't you go down to the grotto and dig for another one?"

Eschon's eyes went cold and he slammed his fist into the bedding. "Okay, Thand, enough of the self-pity. I'm tired of it. Since you've found that feather, you've become secretive, self-centered, and hostile."

"I just want to be left alone, Eschon. Why can't you accept that?"

"Because it's not you. This sickness that you have is in your head. The power you hoped to have is corrupting your thinking. Stop obsessing on what you could do with the feather and start thinking about what you can do to help Elingale. Pretend you never found it. Go down to the grotto. Talk to the people. They miss you."

"I can't leave the house. It's not safe."

"Safe? When hasn't Elingale been safe? If you're talking about protecting your precious feather, I already know that it is buried in a box under your bed."

Thand jumped up and pushed his brother in the chest. "How do you know that? Have you been spying on me?"

"Kin, we're brothers; we have spent our whole lives together. We can't hide secrets from each other. The box and key that Princess Sharman gave you is missing from the table. I assume it's under the floor board, but I don't know for sure."

"Just leave me alone. Okay?"

Eschon threw up his hands. "Wake up, Thand," he said in a fed-up voice and then walked out, shaking his head.

<h1 style="text-align:center">Chapter 17</h1>

CAYMAN WATCHED AS the tropic sun lifted warm, moist air from the ocean and formed towering, vertical clouds called cumulus. Then, just like he had predicted, the massive clouds turned dark and ominous.

The ship continued drifting west as the sailors lashed anything that might wash overboard. The captain ordered extra rope to be issued, and everyone was advised to double up on their life-lines. All nonessential people, including Princess Sharman, were ordered below deck.

Cayman was told to stand alongside the helmsman, while Captain Boreas and Oden stood to the other side. The four men watched as the turquoise sea turned steely gray. Rapidly, the air became thick and the temperature dropped. A dark line of clouds formed in the shape of knuckles. Without warning, the storm raced across the water at the speed of a knockout punch.

A mountain of moist air slammed into the sails. The *Trident Seas* wailed in protest and bucked wildly, but survived the initial impact.

Above their heads, the fabric of the heavens seemed to tear open as a flash of light split the sky and a thunderous boom shook the bones of every sailor.

Waves washed over the deck, seeking to drag the ship to the bottom. From the sea and sky, the assault on the *Trident Seas* continued. Lightning ripped through the clouds, continuing to flash like cannon fire. Anyone still on the deck crouched behind anything solid and gripped their life lines.

A long burst of devil's lightning lit up the sea to reveal a forty-foot wave breaking on top of them. It hit the ship with such force that the rope lashing around some barrels snapped and the casks began rolling wildly across the deck. A sailor, blinded by the rain, was about to be crushed. Oden jumped from the quarter-deck and raced toward him.

A second wave broadsided the ship, and when the foamy wash cleared, both men were gone.

Everyone stood frozen in place. But Cayman flashbacked to the days in his village and the manhood initiations. He recalled watching his friend stop in the middle of the river to kick at the biting piranha fish. A moment later, the boy had been pulled under. He remembered running to the river to save his friend, but his father had grabbed him before he could dive in. "There is nothing you can do, son. He is not strong enough to be one of us." Cayman never forgave his father for not letting him at least try.

Oden was visible about fifty yards from the ship, smacking the water like a drowning man. Cayman untied his lifeline from the railing and plunged into the wrathful sea, the rope trailing. He lost sight of Oden immediately, but a moment later, the first mate reappeared on top of a wave, only to vanish again.

Cayman kept swimming in the general direction of the last sighting. A large wave lifted him, and incredibly, Oden was floundering at the bottom of the wave. Cayman dropped down the face of the wave, but before he could reach him, Oden had disappeared beneath the water.

Cayman dove deep, the salt water stinging his eyes. The storm had reduced the underwater visibility to a few feet. He swam deeper until he thought his lungs would explode. Nothing. Fighting the impulse to breathe, he surfaced.

Lightning lit the dark sea, revealing Oden a hundred yards away, coughing and spitting and doing everything he could to keep his head above water.

Cayman swam like a dolphin toward Oden, but Oden slipped under once again. Knowing it was unlikely that the first mate would resurface, Cayman followed him down. He swam beneath the murky water, looking in all directions. A dark object to his right caught his attention, and he scissor-kicked several times, then reached out. He touched hair and grabbed on. Several swift kicks later, he surfaced with an unconscious Oden. Cayman turned Oden about, wrapped his powerful arms around the drowning man's chest and began pumping the water out of his lungs. Treading water with the burden of extra weight was exhausting, but the other choice would be to let Oden drown. He continued the compressions until he felt a tremor and Oden began coughing up water.

"What's happening?" Oden choked out.

Cayman tied the loose end of the rope around Oden's chest. "Just try to keep your chin above the water. I'll be right back."

He set off swimming toward a bobbing barrel. The wind worked against him and pushed the barrel away. He remembered his ordeal and how the far side of the river had never seemed to get closer. *Keep swimming.* Finally, his fingertips touched the cask. He untied the rope from his waist and secured it to the barrel. Then, pulling the line hand over hand, he brought Oden to the barrel. Oden saw the barrel and grabbed on like a newborn to his mother.

Through chattering teeth, Oden said, "I can't believe you did this. You're insane, but I owe my life to you."

"Save the gratitude. We're not out of danger yet."

A wave lifted them high enough to see the ship in the distance. Cayman was a powerful swimmer, but in these conditions, no one was strong enough to swim that far. They looked at each other and knew the ship could not be turned around. In a storm like this, an overboard sailor was as good as gone.

They dropped into a water trough, and when they rose back up, they could see the ship's sails had gone limp. Strangely, the upper part of the storm continued driving the clouds in the direction of Skull Island. Once again, they dropped below the sight line, then surged back up. The wind had returned and the sails began to billow. But the air was coming from the opposite direction. It was as if the storm had split itself in half, the upper part pushing east and the lower portion west.

Soon, the reversed surface winds flattened the waves and calmed the sea, making it possible to attempt a rescue. The two half-drowned men waved excitedly when they saw a longboat lowered to the sea.

Back on board, Cayman helped Oden limp across the deck. The sailors began to clap. They had misjudged the newest member of the crew. Captain Boreas, ashen-faced, stood at his door and waved them in.

Shivering, the two men stood in front of Boreas while water dripped into pools beneath their feet. A rare look of fear and confusion was on the captain's face. He had lost one man and nearly two more. His eyes darted from one to the other as if they might have an answer for the nature of this storm.

The captain stammered, "That, that was the most disturbing thing I have ever experienced. The magic protecting this island is stronger than anything I've seen. We would've been annihilated if we had landed. I'm not going to risk our lives again trying to find a ghost." He lowered his chin to his chest. In a defeated voice, he said, "Turn the ship around. Chart a new course."

87

Chapter 18

BAYLOCK ROSE WITH the sun, eager to start his search for the Kookachoo Bird.

The warm sunshine and fresh salt breeze enhanced his buoyant mood. A rare smile crossed his face. *The puzzle is almost solved. Before long I'll have the feather, and soon thereafter, I'll be master of all. I'll settle an old score and start my conquest with Adriana Island. They'll be given no mercy. King Treutlen and Enunciation will see what real power looks like.*

For the next half hour, he observed the sky and watched the trees. Seagulls and pelicans flew high above the island, but no other birds were visible. He frowned. *Why did I think that this was going to be easy?*

From over his shoulder, a bird with a long tail feather sailed past. His pulse quickened as he put a spyglass to his eye. The bird came to rest on a tree branch, twisting its head in all directions. The feathers were white with black vertical stripes. He shook his head disappointedly. He needed red with a long white feather.

He looked to the sky again and realized the sky was not shimmering as usual. The intensity of his project had caused him to neglect the island's defenses. A quick mental scan revealed that the repulse spell surrounding the island had weakened.

Something must have happened to drain the energy. He reenergized the force field with an incantation:

"Energy of Earth, hear my call.
Surround this island,
Protecting it from all."

The upper air began to shimmer once again, and since he was not immune to the assault of snakes, spiders, and other deadly creatures, he revived a similar ward for himself.

There were a few copses of trees on the east side where he might spot some birds. As he walked in that direction, he noticed there wasn't the usual quantity of bones lying around. Maybe the security system was too efficient. That would explain the lack of birds flying onto the island. The repulse spell was keeping them away. He was wasting time looking for the exotic bird on Skull Island.

Walking back toward the skull, he recalled that there were people living on a nearby isle called Raintree Island. Maybe they would know more about the bird. A change of scenery would be welcomed after spending all of those days penned up in his cave.

Baylock hoisted the sail on his repaired boat and maneuvered through the treacherous coral reef. As he turned to the south, he looked back at his creation. No one would guess that behind the two eyes of the skull were his laboratory and library and behind the nose was his sleeping quarters. He looked at the cave entrance. If the head didn't frighten the intruders and they were skillful enough to maneuver past the coral reef, he had engineered a gate that looked like a jawbone rising out of the water. The illusion of being swallowed by the skull should stop them.

He turned his attention to sailing. Keeping the coastline on his portside, he travelled to the furthest point on the island and then crossed the channel to Raintree Island. Twenty minutes later, he rounded a crooked finger of land and entered the bay. He was expecting to see other ships, but the harbor was unoccupied. *Good. Less people, less distractions.*

After dropping anchor, the wizard climbed a steep trail into the steamy jungle, passing two empty shacks. Farther down the footpath, he came to a small community. The inhabitants appeared to make their living by repairing ships. It seemed like the perfect location for this type of business. The abundant trees could be harvested and made into ship planking and sailing masts. Tree sap could be gathered and made into pitch, the sticky substance that made boats waterproof.

Baylock looked into the valley and saw a rangy boy of about twelve years skinning the bark off a fallen tree. The wizard threw a pebble at the boy to get his attention, and then he waved for the boy to come up.

The boy's eyes narrowed but he put down his axe and walked toward Baylock.

"Yes, sir, how can I help?"

Baylock pulled out his book and held it up.

"Do you know what this is, boy?"

"Of course I do. It's a book."

"Good," he said as he opened it. "Have you ever seen this bird?"

The boy sounded out the syllables "Koo-ka-choo," then recognized the name. "I've heard the legend but I've never seen one. They say the person who finds the white feather will become rich and powerful."

"I know the legend, but I'm trying to find out where the bird might live."

"Men passing through have said they've seen the bird, but I don't know if it's true or just sailors bragging."

Baylock scowled. "Is there anything besides rumors that you can tell me about this bird? Has it ever been seen around here?"

"No, sir. I told you I've never seen one, so that's about it."

Baylock swore and then mumbled, "A complete waste of time."

He started to walk away, and then remembered he hadn't tested his latest spell. He called the young man back and tossed a pinch of dust on the boy.

"Worthless is a word and now it's unheard," chanted the wizard.

The startled boy coughed, and when the vapor cleared, Baylock said, "Do as I command. Say, 'I am worthless.'"

The boy opened his mouth but only grunted.

"Good. Now tell me your name."

A high-pitched sound came from the boy's mouth, but no words. His eyes protruded as he tried again. A squeak was all that came out. His breathing became more rapid as he tried once more. Nothing again. The young man seemed to be mute.

Distraught, the boy made a guttural roar and started pounding his fist on Baylock's chest. He pointed to his mouth, made gestures of frustration, and then began to cry.

Baylock slowly shook his head. *Two very precious elements wasted, for nothing.* He began to walk back toward his boat, but the boy kept tugging on his arm.

The wizard pushed him to the ground and said, "Sorry, kid, but we both lost today."

Chapter 19

IT HAD BEEN almost a week since Thand had fallen out of the tree, and all he was able to do was think about the feather. He had lost a noticeable amount of weight, and dark circles had formed under his eyes. Frequent headaches began to plague him, and sleep was elusive. To add to his pathetic look, he had worn the same clothes for many days, and the smell was becoming annoying. Fishing and visits to the grotto seemed a thing of the past.

In an effort to please his mother, Thand came out of his room and sat down for breakfast. He pushed the food around his plate but barely ate more than a few scraps. Just as he was standing up to go back to his room, Eschon clasped a hand on his arm and said, "Maybe the solution to your problem lies in one of those books in Creedy's library. After all, they helped you solved the dragon bone mystery. Let's get out of here and find out."

Thand put a hand on his forehead and said, "Maybe tomorrow. Right now I have a hammering headache."

After Eschon left for the day, Thand moved his bed aside, took up a floor plank, and removed the feather from a half-buried box. He turned toward the window, held the feather up to the light, and began speaking. "I'm going mad trying to make sense of this. Is it possible that the Kookachoo Bird thinks I am unworthy and removed the power? Some people think the Elwins are inferior. Or is it possible that I wasn't meant to find the feather?"

He held the feather up to the window light and pondered the question.

"Was Princess Sharman supposed to discover it instead of me? It was lying on the trail that led to her ship. We were so busy talking to each other that it's possible we passed by without seeing it."

Suddenly, the door creaked open and Eschon walked in. Thand turned swiftly, hiding the feather behind his back.

Eschon threw a book on the bed. "Read this. There might be something in it you can use." Without another word, he walked out of the room.

Did he see the feather? Thand had told Eschon that the feather was hidden somewhere else in the forest, a spot that only he knew. Thand put the white plume under a blanket, stepped to the door, and peeked out. The house was empty except for his mother, and she was busy, as usual, cooking food.

Thand shrugged his shoulders. *I guess not.*

He walked back to the bed, picked up the book, and read the title: *The Power of Magic.* At once his hands began to tingle and the headache vanished.

He pushed a chair in front of the door and then sat on the bed. Placing the feather across his lap, he began to read. There were spells of love and some for beauty. Spells for fire and spells for rain. But his pulse quickened when he found a chapter devoted to wealth.

All that day he tried various chants that referred to power or wealth. By nightfall, his frustration had returned, as well as the headache. He looked out the window and saw the setting sun. Knowing that Eschon would be coming home for dinner soon, he closed the book and returned the room to its normal look. When Eschon asked if the book was of any help, Thand replied, "Useless."

In the morning, after Eschon had left to go fishing, Thand brought the feather out. Once again, he picked up the book. It was just before midday when he found a section that discussed magic and feathers.

Thand had begun to talk to the feather out loud. "What should I ask you to do?"

He looked out the window to a field of corn. It looked wilted, which reminded Thand that they had not had rain in over a month. He went back to the book and found a chant to make it rain. He pointed the feather toward the sky and read the words:

> "Feather of bird,
> Feather of might,
> Rain clouds, thunderclouds, now unite."

Nothing happened. "Gotterslamit! How does this work?"

About fifteen minutes later he heard a far-off rumble. It was thunder. Ten minutes after that, it began to rain.

He ran outside and danced in the rain. "It works. It works."

Back inside, dripping water on the floor, he pointed the feather and asked for the rain to stop. But it continued. "Well, I haven't found a chant yet for stopping rain."

He heard Eschon talking to his mother. Hiding the feather under his bed, he went to the kitchen and told Eschon he was ready to go to Creedy's library.

Eschon's eyes widened. "All right, let's go now. It just stopped raining."

A few raindrops dripped from the oak tree as they walked toward the mansion.

"Eschon, you might not believe it, but I just used the feather to make it rain and then ordered it to stop."

Eschon looked skeptical. "Yeah, right. Make something happen now and I'll believe you."

"I don't have the feather right now. As soon as we get back home, I'll do it. Right now, I want to see if there are any more books on magic and also show you the secret escape way in Creedy's bedroom."

"Okay, I never did see how he got out of the house. This will be fun."

Once inside, Thand led the way up, taking two stairs at a time. "The trapdoor is inside of the closet. I'll show you."

Thand opened the door and noticed a bag of coins sitting on the floor. He took a step back and sucked in a quick breath. "Look, Eschon, a bag of money. Now do you believe me?"

Chapter 20

PRINCESS SHARMAN HAD followed the captain's order and remained in her cabin during the fearsome gale. When the storm first started, she thought it wouldn't be too dangerous, but the motion became so violent that she had a change of mind. To fight off panic, she thought back to Thand and her teaching days in Elingale. It had been the most rewarding time of her life.

As the ship heaved back and forth, she thought about the young children and their enthusiasm for learning. If the kids had their way, she would have been teaching twenty-four hours a day. She thought about their laughter and the silly jokes, and despite the danger of the storm, she smiled. Nothing but good would come from their learning.

The storm began to lessen. At least she could get up and walk around the room. She decided to begin a letter to Thand. It had only been four days and so much had changed since they parted. He probably thought that she was back in her castle and sleeping in a feather bed.

Not too long after the storm subsided, there was a knock on her cabin door. *Cayman?*

When she opened the door, Oden was standing there frowning,

soggy from head to toe. She was surprised by the sight and invited him in. Oden ignored her request and explained what had taken place while she was safe in her cabin.

She grabbed his hands and said, "I'm so sorry. Thank goodness you're okay."

"I'm not finished speaking," he said, and then he repeated the captain's order to turn back home immediately.

"No! Oden, you can't let him do this," the princess cried. "Uncle Warmund is out there somewhere, waiting for our help. You didn't give up on me when I was lost. Why give up on him?"

"This isn't my decision. I'm just following orders. He says we're chasing—"

"Don't you dare refer to my uncle as a ghost," she said defiantly. "Until someone can prove he's gone, I won't give up searching for him."

A vein pulsed in Oden's neck. One person had drowned and nearly two more. He leaned forward toward Sharman. "The captain's order is not open for discussion." He turned and walked away.

The princess, stinging from Oden's comment, flopped on her bed. Her lips were pressed tight and her eyes fixed on the ceiling. *I may not have the power to turn the ship around, but when I get home, I'll tell Father that Thand and I will search on our own.*

That night she fell into a fitful sleep. A muffled shout made her think that pirates boarded her ship. Then the far-off sounds of battle alarmed her. She turned to see what was happening, but her eyes wouldn't open. Suddenly, the cabin wall splintered into long shards of wood. Her vision cleared and she tried to jump out of bed. But her legs felt like a huge boulder was lying on top, pinning her down. A hooked-nose pirate with a jutting chin stepped through the shattered mess, swinging his sword.

He stopped in midstride when he saw her. The surprised look on his face changed slowly to a lustful smile.

She screamed, "Help! Uncle Warmund, I need you." But the words sounded like she was underwater.

The pirate's eyes darted around the room as if searching for someone else. Then he put his sword back in its scabbard and walked toward her, one foot dragging.

Her breathing became shallow and she tried to run, but there was no feeling in her legs. As the pirate came closer, she put her palms out, hoping to keep him from touching her. Dark smudges of gunpowder smeared his red jacket. The unwashed smell of his body repulsed her. He reached out and placed his cold clammy hands on either side of her face.

Where's Thand? Why isn't he here to save me?

His breath was rancid. His teeth were yellow and wolf-like. He opened his mouth as if to bite her.

She screamed and jolted into the sitting position, hugging her pillow. Her eyes darted around the room. The rising sun was visible through the window. "A dream," she said to no one. "Only a frightful dream."

She rolled out of bed; there was nothing wrong with her legs. The cabin walls were as solid as ever. She pulled off her damp clothes and changed into a pale yellow blouse and brown leather pants. Lacing up her boots, she thought, *This room is too confining. I've got to get out of here.*

Stepping into the fresh air, she took a deep breath. Oden's comment about growing up still bothered her. Out of the corner of her eye, she noticed some sailors watching her, studying her. She looked down at herself. In her haste to leave the room she had not properly fastened her shirt.

She blushed, turned her back to the men, and finished buttoning the garment. She looked herself over. *My pants are a little shorter and maybe the buttons on my blouse pull more than they should, but clothes shrink over time.* She examined herself again. *Or maybe I am no longer a child?*

The large, square-rigged *Trident Seas* turned smoothly into the mouth of the Empeerean River. The ship buzzed with excitement, as it usually did whenever the vessel returned to home port.

The incoming tide was pushing them smoothly toward town. Sailors lined the yardarms, looking sharp in their dark blue trousers with matching shirts. Around their necks, various colored scarfs set them apart by rank and duty. Captain Boreas, wearing his usual crisp blue jacket and white pants, stood beside the helm. His eyes seemed to be staring straight ahead, but the sailors knew they were everywhere at once.

Along the port side of the ship, the grain fields were ripe. Their stalks lined up like soldiers in formation. Willow trees bordered the right bank, waving a greeting with their slender branches. As the waterway narrowed, the captain ordered the sails to be furled. Minutes later, Empeerean, the most important city of Adrianna Island, coasted into sight.

The helmsman expertly steered the ship toward the dock. At the captain's command, thick ropes went flying over the side to the waiting workmen, and with swift precision, the ship was tethered to the pier.

Unconcerned by the activity on the main deck, Princess Sharman went through her sea chest, looking for the proper attire for arrival in Empeerean. A skirt and blouse were more appropriate than her leather pants and shirt. After trying on several combinations, she settled on her white silk tunic and forest-green skirt.

She pinched the bridge of her nose and squeezed her eyes

tight. Her mood had been sour ever since the captain had abandoned her uncle. She reminded herself to calm down and try to relax. A grouchy face in public was not allowed.

She took a deep breath, brushed the green skirt once more, pushed her long, auburn hair behind her shoulders, and pasted a happy smile on her face.

When she stepped onto the gangplank, the crowd roared. An honor guard lined both sides of a red carpet. King Treutlen and her mother, Queen Twila, stood waiting in front of the royal coach.

The overdone pomp and ceremony was proceeding just as expected. The King's Guards were dressed in royal-blue surcoats with golden-hilt broadswords fastened to their hips. In their left hands they clutched green metal shields painted with the Royal Emblem—a lion facing a unicorn. Sunlight glinted off the soldiers' polished steel helmets festooned with black crests made of horsehair.

Funny, she thought, *most of the world would love to live in a palace, but it seems too contrived, too safe—everything on a schedule. Life on Lapis Lazuli was much more exciting.*

She picked up the hem of her skirt and stepped off. A gust of wind swept a strand of hair into her eye.

Twang.

She felt a sharp pain, like a knife stabbing her neck. The force knocked her backward and the sky went black.

Chapter 21

THOSE AROUND PRINCESS Sharman heard a *thwack*, then a startled groan.

The crowd went silent; her parents' faces turned white as Princess Sharman arched backward, her knees buckled, and she toppled off the gangplank onto the pier.

The throng pushed forward to see what had happened, but the guards did their job and held everyone back. Her parents rushed forward. King Treutlen dropped to the ground and put his hand under her head. The fletched arrow shaft protruding from her neck turned his stomach. Sharman looked at him with a vacant stare, and then her eyes rolled back inside of her head.

With tears rolling down his cheeks, the king carefully scooped his limp daughter against his chest and stood. "Sharman, wake up. Please wake up and talk to me. You're going to be all right. I promise."

He ran toward the carriage screaming, "Get back! Don't touch her," to anyone who tried to assist. Gently, he placed her inside. A red stain was spreading across her white top. The shaft had entered her left shoulder, near the base of her neck.

The king's physician, Medicina, was a standard part of the entourage. She elbowed her way to the coach and begged the queen's pardon as she stepped inside and began to examine the princess. She listened to her heart and then tore part of her shirt away so she could examine the wound.

"It would have been better if the arrow had passed all the way through, but it glanced off her shoulder bone first. Luckily, the bleeding isn't major. Another inch and it would have severed the main blood vessel in her neck. Hopefully, her unconsciousness is a result of the fall. I must remove the arrowhead and shaft as soon as possible."

The physician took a folded cloth out of her bag and pressed it around the entry point of the arrow. She looked up to the king with sad eyes.

"You've seen this kind of wound before. You know how dangerous and painful it is to remove the shaft. It must be done in a restricted location, not the back seat of the coach."

"You're right," he said in a faltering voice filled with pain. "I'll ride back to the castle and prepare a room."

Without another word spoken, he leaped onto a nearby horse, wheeled it around, and galloped toward the palace. A squad of his elite soldiers raced behind him in a vain attempt to catch up.

Queen Twila squeezed her hips into the coach. She removed the physician's hand from the bandage and replaced it with her own. Medicina was not offended; she also was a mother.

The queen leaned down to kiss her forehead and then jolted up. "She isn't breathing!"

The assassin cursed his luck as he slid down the roof and dropped onto the second-story porch. He scanned the vicinity—empty. Anyone within several blocks of the waterfront had rushed to the disturbance.

He descended to the ground where his partner was waiting with a horse. "Did you see anyone while I was on the roof?"

"A woman came out of the tavern, but she was hurrying to the kitchen house. I don't think she saw anything."

"You better be right," the assassin said, poking his finger in his chest. "We can't have any witnesses."

"I'm telling you, we're okay. I'll meet you tomorrow." The accomplice ran toward the docks, hoping to blend in with the crowd.

The killer swore again. Despite his high-powered bow, a gust of wind had ruined his shot. But he had taken a precaution and poisoned the arrow tip. If the wound didn't kill her, the toxin would. And if that didn't work, he would find another way to finish the job and collect the other half of a substantial bounty.

Chapter 22

KING TREUTLEN GALLOPED toward the gleaming white walls of the castle, racing across the wooden bridge and passing the two stone lions. He came to a quick stop in front of the Great Hall, jumped from his horse, and began to bark orders. The servants ran in every direction as they set about making preparations for the arrival of the royal coach.

He walked in circles, waiting. *How did this happen? This wasn't an accident. Who would want to kill my daughter? Where is Oden? He needs to find the person responsible for this.*

As if on cue, Oden and his horse thundered across the bridge at breakneck speed. He slid off the back of the horse while it was still moving forward. He ran to the king, sweat rolling down his face.

"The carriage will be here in a few minutes. I don't know where the arrow came from, but I'll find out."

"Get your best men, go back into town, and start asking questions. Tell the people the worst has happened. I don't want the assassin to think he failed, otherwise he may try again."

Inside Sharman's bedroom, the king's physician, Medicina, removed the blood-soaked shirt and looked at the wound once again. The swollen skin around the arrow had turned purplish-red. She looked back over her shoulder to the worried king and queen.

"I am concerned that the princess has still not regained consciousness. If this was caused by a simple bump on the head, she would be awake by now." She noticed a circle forming around the lesion. "This is not a simple arrow wound. My guess is that the arrow tip was poisoned."

Twila's knees buckled but the king steadied her. Medicina looked back toward her patient but continued, "As you know, the pain of removal is considerable. It will have to be pushed through the shoulder muscles and out the back. For this reason, it's good that she is unconscious. However, if she wakes. . . Well, you just might be better off to go ahead and leave.

"Ridiculous," said the king.

Queen Twila stood next to her daughter and patted her fevered brow with a cool cloth. "I wish I could change places with her."

The physician directed her assistants to stand behind the princess and press down on her shoulder.

"Then don't be surprised if she starts screaming."

The arrow had been safely removed, but Princess Sharman wasn't getting any better. The night was passing painfully slow. King Treutlen paced around the edges of the room, clutching his arms to his chest, while the queen watched helplessly. The princess moaned softly as her brow became dangerously hot. The exhausted queen pursed her lips together and placed another cool towel on her daughter's head. It was the only thing she knew to do.

The king was trying not to snap under the pressure. But this was his only daughter, the future queen, and she seemed very near to death. He became light-headed and put his hand against the wall. A shadow passed in front of his eyes. Outwardly he didn't acknowledge the spirit world, but inwardly he felt it existed. He blinked. There was nothing there; however, a foul odor lingered. *Was it the stagnant air*, he thought, *or the shade of death?* He shook his head vigorously and then left the room.

"Has anyone been out here?" he said to the guard.

"No, Your Grace."

The boy seemed alert. He believed him. "I want another guard to stand at the end of the hallway."

"Two guards. Yes, Your Grace."

When he returned, the queen was asleep in her chair. The king shook his head and went to Sharman's bedside. Blood-tinged sweat was oozing from her forehead. His mouth flew open.

He clipped Twila on the shoulder and bellowed, "What kind of a mother are you? How can you sleep at a time like this? Look, she's sweating blood!"

He flew to the door and yelled for the guard to find the physician and bring her back at once. "Pull her off the chamber pot if necessary, but I want her here immediately."

Treutlen kept circling the room, rolling his hands in a ball and repeating, "I must find a way. I must find a way."

A moment later, the door swung open and Medicina ran in. The physician pulled back the sheets covering the Princess. Without hesitation, she ordered the queen to remove all of the princess' garments. The queen's hand flew to her chest. "Who are you to command the queen?"

"Do as you're told, Twila, and keep your pompous mouth closed," yelled the king.

Medicina flinched and then raised her own voice. "Guard, go to the springhouse and bring back buckets of cold water. Keep bringing them until I tell you to stop."

She turned to the king. "You're under tremendous strain. Maybe you should leave. I am doing all that a doctor is trained to do."

"And that's the problem," he cried out. "Your conventional methods aren't working. My poor daughter is wasting away in front of my eyes, and all you do is put wet rags around her. There is only one thing left to do. I just hope that I haven't waited too long."

Chapter 23

THE KING PUSHED hard on the double doors that led to his bedroom suite. Normally, he would have sent a carrier bird. But there was no time for that. He turned, locked the doors behind him, and hurried to a concealed panel inside his bedroom. He found the decorative medallion that was slightly off-color and pressed on it. The ornament receded into the wooden panel, and a narrow, five-foot section of the wall descended into the floor.

Without waiting for the wall to fully recede, he stepped over it and pressed another button inside the room. The panel reversed and sealed him inside.

An aqua-blue orb in the ceiling began to shimmer. The cerulean light's intensity grew until it was as bright as the sun. Shadows ceased to exist.

A table with several playing cards lying on top was the only item in the room. He walked over and picked up the cards. This was not an ordinary set of playing cards. There were only five, and each one was hand-carved out of a rare, rose-colored wood.

King Treutlen spread the cards on the table, picked out a specific card, and studied it closely. Staring back at him was the etched image of a thin man with a long beard that grew down to his chest. The artist's engraved detail had even included the thick, round glasses that gave his face the appearance of an owl. Treutlen looked intently at the wooden card. It was the face of the Great Wizard Enunciation.

The card was ice-cold to the touch, but once the king began to concentrate all of his attention on the card, it became warm. Blue sparks danced on the corner of the card, and then slowly, the wooden portrait faded into the real face of Enunciation.

"It is not good when we have to communicate this way," said the somber-looking wizard. "What's the problem?"

"Sharman is gravely ill. She has been shot by an arrow— a poison arrow, I think. She is unconscious and sweating what looks to be blood. I need your help; what can you do?"

"I have some medicines here that I can send—"

"No! There's no time for that. I need you here, with the medicines, immediately."

"That would mean—"

"I know what it means. Just do it."

"I'm not sure if I can. It's been a long time. I'm an old man now."

"You must. There's no choice. Her life depends on this."

"Then I'll be there after dark."

"Why so late?"

"You know why. You just forgot."

Late that evening there was a great commotion around the king's castle. Horses kicked at their stalls, barnyard animals dashed around in circles, and stable boys ran for cover. Only a few of the veteran soldiers understood what was happening.

Out of the darkness, a torrent of wind suddenly swept across the paddock, a roar of fire lit the sky, and a red-scaled dragon touched down in a nearby field. Oden ran to the dragon's side and greeted the Great Wizard Enunciation. Showing no fear of the dragon, Oden began unbuckling the straps that held Enunciation in the saddle.

"It's been a long time since I've seen you on that dragon. How was the ride?"

The wizard's knees buckled as he touched the ground. Oden put his arm around his side to help support him.

"Leave me alone. I'm fine. It's just that it's been a whirlwind since I got the king's message. Packing my medicines and potions, worrying about the princess, and then I had to hunt for the words that call the dragon back to the castle. It's been so long since I've ridden her, and I wasn't sure if she would come. Now, stop fussing over me and get me to the princess."

The king was at the lower castle door waiting impatiently as Enunciation hobbled forward. He put his arm around the wizard, embraced him, and then placed his hand under the wizard's elbow to help him move along more quickly.

Enunciation shook off the king's arm. "Leave me alone. I'm not crippled. You'd be walking the same way if you just spent two hours flying through the night on a dragon."

Despite his anxiety, a slight smile cracked the king's face. *Still as feisty as ever.*

"Since talking to you earlier, the blood-sweat has stopped, but now her face has swollen like a puffer fish," the king said as they hurried to Sharman's room.

Medicina was waiting in the room and stood. Quickly, she updated the wizard on the princess' condition. He removed the bandage and looked at her shoulder. The wound was red and inflamed. Yellow-white pus oozed from the center. A black loop nearly encircled the lesion.

"If it were just an arrow wound, I could heal it in a matter of minutes. It's far worse," Medicina said in a rush of words.

Enunciation unpacked a large urn of black charcoal powder and a tiny glass vile that contained a green balm. Several bandages with the fragrance of cinnamon were placed at the princess' side.

"See this black ring circling around the wound?" the wizard said. "It's a sign of a magically enhanced poison. When both ends meet, she will die. Now please, stand back."

He heard whispering behind his back and looked up to see everyone staring at him.

"Out! Everyone get out. This is not a tournament ring."

The king and queen were used to these fits of temper from Enunciation and did as he asked. But Medicina ignored his order.

The wizard removed the bandages and then reached over for the black powder. The physician was still there, watching him intently.

He stopped and glared at Medicina. "You too. I don't share my secrets."

Chapter 24

THE TWO BROTHERS were sitting in their bedroom counting coins. "I told you, Eschon, I made the wish when I first found the feather. There's nothing that says it has to appear right in front of me."

"I'm just saying rain storms pop up all the time and Creedy could have forgotten the bag during his quick escape."

Suddenly, there was commotion in the front room. They could hear Treelore's voice, and she was excited about something. Thand stepped out of his room and Treelore gushed. "*Trident Seas* is dropping anchor. Maybe Princess Sharman's returned."

Without replying, Thand turned and ran toward the beach. Halfway down the trail, he encountered Oden.

"Thand, I'm glad you're here. I was just coming to see you."

Oden looked like he had aged ten years, but Thand didn't want to insult his friend. "How's the Princess? Is she with you? Is she okay?"

Oden put his arm around Thand's shoulder. "Are you okay? You look like you've been ill."

"Well, now that you say it, you don't look so good yourself. What's happening? Is Princess Sharman okay?

"No. I'm afraid not. She is in grave health."

"What do you mean? What's wrong with her?"

"She was shot by an arrow as she was departing the ship in Empeerean and has been unconscious ever since. She's being cared for by a doctor but—"

"Then I must go back to be by her side."

"That would be great. I think you're the dose of medicine she needs. The Great Wizard Enunciation is with her now, trying to work his magic and keep her alive."

Without thinking, Thand turned toward the longboat, but Oden grabbed his shoulder. "What are you doing, Thand? We just can't turn around and sail away. The tide won't change until late tonight, so the ship's going nowhere until then."

Thand looked toward the ship and then back at Oden. "You're right. What am I thinking? Let's go back to the house, and I'll tell everyone I'm leaving."

Grace smiled when she saw Oden. "How are you? Is everyone well at the castle?"

"Mom, not now. This is not a social call. Something serious has happened to Princess Sharman." Thand gave a quick version of what he had just heard and headed toward his room.

Eschon absorbed what had been said and grabbed his brother's shoulder. "Don't leave yet. I'm going with you."

Thand stopped abruptly, surprised by the words. "Aren't you afraid of sailing? I thought you wouldn't leave Mother."

"I guess I was afraid of leaving and sailing too far into the ocean. What if I couldn't get home? I was afraid of being around so many strangers. I thought protecting Mother was a good excuse to hide my fears. But, after you came back, I promised that if I ever got a second chance, I'd join you."

Grace gripped the back of the chair when she heard those words. Her lips began to tremble. "You can't go. I hate when the family is split. Besides, what if they come and take me away again? I'm scared."

"I understand," Thand said in a soothing tone. "Locked up in Creedy's dungeon for weeks had to be terrible. But, Mom, Lord Creedy is gone...forever."

"Where's Baylock? He might return," Grace said as her eyes darted from boy to boy.

"There's no one to worry about. The whole island has been checked, and he's not here. With Lord Creedy gone, he has no reason to come back. Besides, the villagers will care for you, and the king's soldiers will protect you."

Eschon took his mother's hand. "I have to leave this island someday if I'm to learn about the rest of the world. This would be a good time to start. Besides, Thand will need my help finding the person who tried to murder Princess Sharman."

"Don't say murder. She isn't dead yet," scolded Thand. Then he walked over to his mother and gave her a hug. "I'll talk to Treelore and the villagers. I'll let them know you're here by yourself. I'm sure that there won't be a day that goes by without someone checking to see how you're doing. And if I know the Elwins, you'll have more food in this house than three of us could eat."

Thand waited nervously for a response while Eschon chewed on his lip and looked at the ceiling.

"Does anyone want a cup of tea?" she asked, biding her time. "How about something to eat? Oden, you must be hungry."

"Yes. I'll never turn down that offer."

She wiped her nose. "I knew this day was coming. If your father were still alive, this would be easier on me. But he's not. I still think of you two as children. I guess I'm just fooling myself. I know there's more to the world than this island. It's wishful thinking to believe Elingale could hold you here."

Thand crossed his arms impatiently. He knew this speech and was anxious to get to Princess Sharman. *Come on, Mom. I have to get out of here.*

"There's an old saying that mothers must give their children roots and wings. Your roots are well planted here in Elingale, but I guess it's time that I give you your wings."

Thand watched Eschon's taut face melt into a wide grin, and then Eschon gave his mother a hug.

Thand's impatience was growing. "It's a long trip back to Adrianna Island, Mother. We need to get going." He motioned Eschon toward the bedroom.

Both boys were excited as they gathered their meager belongings. Grace called to the boys: "Finish up. Eat while the food is hot."

That quick, Grace had put a small feast on the table. Oden joined them. The subject of the princess was ignored, as if talking about her condition would make it worse. Instead, Oden talked about the search for Uncle Warmund and the strange magic of Skull Island.

Thand was barely listening and repeatedly looked out the window, watching the sun descend, knowing the tide would start to change at sunset.

"Isn't it time we stop talking and go to the ship?" asked Thand.

"Don't be rude," admonished Grace. "I'm sure Oden knows when it's the proper time to leave."

"Unfortunately, he is right," said Oden. "I hate to leave your company, Grace, and I'll certainly miss your cooking. As Eschon will soon learn, wonderful food like this doesn't exist on a ship."

Grace stood in the doorway and watched the trio melt into the dark, tears rolling down her cheeks. When they were out of sight, she wiped the apron across her face and turned, twisting her ankle. She reached out to brace herself, but it was too late. The month in Creedy's prison had slowed her reflexes considerably. Her hand dragged across the table as she banged her head and then hit the floor. A second later, a plate of food bounced off the top of her head. Blood trickled down her forehead and mixed with the table scraps.

Chapter 25

BAYLOCK WOKE JUST before dawn. Now that he knew the Kookachoo Bird existed, he just had to find someone who knew where it lived.

The sun had barely lifted itself above the horizon when he set off for Whistler Key. It was a medium-sized island about a half-day sail due east. The island was known for a variety of odd creatures. One of those, he hoped, would be the Kookachoo Bird. In fact, the island's name was derived from a peculiar species of bird that whistled like a teenage boy watching a girl pass by.

Whistler Key had many other bird species, like the orange and black lark that sang a song that sounded like, "Here, here. Come right here."

It was also home to the Kookaburra, a curious bird with a distinct call that sounded like out-of-control laughing.

The magician rounded Skull Island and headed east. Once on the open water, a strong west wind whipped up the waves until they were capped in white. The blustery sea made for a jarring, salt-sprayed ride, but it also meant an early arrival at his destination.

Most of Whistlers Key's history was insignificant. The harbor had once been a simple ship refuge used only to restock fresh water and make minor repairs. But as trade routes grew, its strategic location transformed it into a significant harbor town. The docks were surrounded with trades that served the numerous needs of the incoming ships.

Baylock chose this busy seaport for a reason. Sailors traveled to many different regions and would be more likely to have seen a variety of strange things. The more sailors he spoke to, the more likely he was to discover the whereabouts of the Kookachoo Bird.

Presently, Baylock could see two ships unloading their goods while five more rode on anchor.

On the left side of the U-shaped harbor, there were warehouses and boat-repair facilities. The center section was lined with a customs house, a rope maker, a woodcarver, and a chandler. Fishmongers, butchers, and beer-sellers filled the remaining space. An open-air market, trading in all sorts of merchandise from practical to curious, operated just beyond the embankment.

Several young boys stood at the jetty waiting for Baylock to throw them his ropes. They tied off his boat and he climbed onto the pier, tossing them a coin for their troubles. On a normal day, the docks would smell like rotting fish, stagnant water, and horse dung mixed with salt air. But right now, a ship was offloading some cargo that perfumed the air with exotic spices of the Far East.

Baylock stood at the edge of town and stared. He pinched the bridge of his nose and sighed. *This is a lot of ground to cover for an impatient man.* He smoothed his wrinkled clothes and began to walk. Within minutes, his shirt was plastered to his damp skin. Humidity and the lack of a sea breeze made the weather oppressive.

All afternoon Baylock walked the docks, talking to the men and asking questions. Finally, the town clock chimed five times.

It had been a long, sweltering day. He collapsed onto a nearby bench and blotted his forehead. He didn't like humidity or people, so this day had been fatiguing. But he had seen some interesting things moving about. There were shirtless men covered in tattoos, jugglers, and sword swallowers. There were even crates of strange animals that were being shipped to a sultan's kingdom. But the only responses he got were shrugs and sideway shaking heads when he asked about the Kookachoo Bird.

Wiping his brow, he looked to the western sky. The sun was only a few hours from setting. A decision had to be made: set sail for Skull Island now or spend the evening.

As much as he would have liked to get away from all of this congestion, there seemed no point in going back to the island without an answer. He stood up and ventured a few blocks from the waterfront. On a tree-lined street, he found a well-kept inn called Gerard's Tavern. After sizing up the place, he made arrangements to spend the night.

A stomach growl reminded him that he hadn't eaten all day. The dining room was in an adjoining room, so he walked to the doorway. It was still early in the evening, so the crowd was a light crowd. He scanned the room and found a spot where his back would be against a wall, but facing the door. He walked over to it and claimed it for himself. It was perfect. From this table, he didn't have to watch his back and could watch the patrons come and go. Hopefully, he could find some new faces to question.

A serving girl came over and he ordered a meal with a glass of wine. He studied the crowd while waiting for his food. The merchant class and their wives filled most of the tables. A server arrived with a platter of roasted lamb and pumpernickel bread. He was laying a napkin across his lap when a man came over and asked him to buy a mug of ale.

Baylock sighed heavily. Interruptions at mealtime were usually not tolerated. Placing his knife on the table, he studied the man. He was average in height with receding white hair and an oversized nose. Judging by his strong upper body, he was probably someone who worked on the docks.

A fake smile flashed across Baylock's face. "And why would I do that?"

"You looks like a man seekin' information," the brazen man said with a husky voice. "I work hard most days and keeps my mouth shut. I hear a lot, and I hear you're askin' about a strange bird. Am I right?"

There was no sense in denying it. He had questioned dozens of people that day.

"Not just a strange bird, but a legendary bird. What do you know?"

The man looked at him through shrewd eyes. "I know information cost doubloons and you look like a man that has a few."

"I'll pay an honest price for the right information, but I won't ask you again. What do you know regarding this bird?"

"It's hard t'speak with a dry throat."

This man was irritating but Baylock needed information. In an aggravated voice, he said, "Order what you want but stop playing games."

"I knew you were a fair man when I laid me eyes on you. My name is Sedgley."

Sedgley's clothes were clean but shabby. He took a seat quickly and ordered a plate of cheese and bread to go with a mug of ale. While waiting for his food, he began to talk.

Baylock was impressed with his knowledge of the various islands. He seemed to have a story for each ship in the harbor.

It was as if he was a sea sponge soaking up every word that was spoken on the dock.

"Not long ago I heard a conversation 'tween an Empeerean sailor and one of the dock hands. The sailor wanted to know how the island got its name. So, they started talking 'bout odd birds. I wasn't really listenin', ya know—I'm not that kind of guy. But I heard the words *Kookachoo Bird*. Now, you heard the legend of that bird, so my ears perked up. The Empeerean sailor said that he'd never really seen the bird but knew of a boy on Lapis Lazuli who had come upon it."

Lapis Lazuli! That bird had been right under my nose, and I didn't know it?

Sedgley saw the look of surprise on Baylock's face. "So, you know the legend of the Kookachoo Bird. Have you found the white feather? Be that why you're so wealthy?"

"I'm wealthy because I'm perceptive."

Baylock studied Sedgley for a moment and concluded that he was a keen observer that could be manipulated with coin.

He sat back in his chair and crossed his arms. "You seem to be bright and ambitious. Any chance you'd be looking for new employment? I need a good sailor and second hand around my workshop. The pay is good, and room and board is free."

Sedgley's eyes grew bright, and without asking any questions, he agreed to take the job.

"Gather your belongings and meet me at the small jetty in the morning."

Chapter 26

ESCHON ARRIVED ON the beach just behind Thand and Oden. It was a starless night, and except for a few gently swaying lanterns, the ship was almost invisible. *Maybe leaving home isn't a great idea*, Eschon thought. *What's it going to be like trapped on that ship for three days?*

The boat had always looked harmless when viewed from land, but now this huge, dark thing, filled with strangers, looked menacing. Eschon took a deep breath and climbed into the longboat. He was used to the canoe-like boats they used for fishing. Holding onto the gunwale, he stared at his feet while two sailors pulled on the oars. No one spoke as the boat slid through the inky darkness.

Eschon's stomach rumbled. *Did I eat something disagreeable?* He looked to his older brother for support, but Thand's blank stare told him he was somewhere else.

They arrived at the side of the boat, and he was told to climb a rope ladder. When he hesitated, the oarsmen told him, "Climb the ladder or swim to shore." This ladder was designed for humans, not Elwins. He struggled up the side and climbed over the rail. His heart was beating rapidly as he looked across the deck. His first thought was that he should have listened to the oarsman and swam back home.

Eschon looked up into the complicated rigging. He was fascinated by the ropes, canvas, and wooden arms. He was going to ask Thand a question when he realized that his brother was not there.

Spinning in a circle, he spotted his brother opening a door. "Wait up," he yelled as he dashed across the deck.

Eschon caught up to his brother and pleaded, "Please don't leave me by myself. I don't know where to go or what to do, and I don't understand anything about how this ship works."

Thand chuckled. "Sorry, my mind was somewhere else. I know what you're feeling. It wasn't long ago that I was standing in this same spot with the same fear. Let's store our gear, and then I'll show you around the ship."

Eschon let out a huge breath. His shoulders relaxed.

Thirty minutes after they went below, they were back on the main deck. Eschon's heart was pumping at full speed. "Tell me everything, kin."

"It's too much to cover all at once, but I'll show you the important things now."

Pointing upwards, Thand said, "There are three masts on the ship: the *main mast,* the *foremast,* and the rear sail that's called the *mizzenmast.* You should remember their names. The more you use the proper terminology, the quicker the sailors will accept you. The front of the ship is called the *bow,* and the rear is the *stern.* The right side of the ship is *starboard,* and the left side is *port.*"

"I'm already confused," said Eschon.

"Now, look waaay up there. The wooden arms that are holding the sails are called *yards,* and the basket at the top—it's the highest part of the ship and used as a lookout for spotting land or other ships. It's called the *crow's nest.*"

Eschon put a hand to his cheek. "How am I supposed to remember all of this?"

"You'll get it in time, but that's enough for now. If you want, you can roam around a little more, but be careful to stay out the sailors' way. Preparing to set sail is a busy time. I'll be in the cabin if you need me."

Eschon looked in wonder. How could something this tall not just topple over and sink? It didn't make sense. The smells were also odd. Not just the briny-sea smell—that, he was used to—but the strange mixture of canvas, sweat, and pitch.

Eschon wandered the deck. He was walking and looking up at the same time when he bumped into a tall, dark-skinned man with red braids of hair. Both seemed perplexed. Eschon squeezed his eyes and then opened them again. He had never seen a man of this color.

"Has the sun burnt your skin?" Eschon asked innocently.

Cayman laughed. "Ya man. Has someone stretched your ears?"

"How did your hair get so curly?" responded Eschon, as if he hadn't heard the question.

"In my country, de sun always shines and de curly hair helps me stay cool."

"But what are those red-colored braids supposed to do, and why do you wear beads in them?"

"Yuh be a curious little fellow. Dey make me look pretty. Now, my turn," said Cayman. "Why are yuh ears pointed? When will yuh grow taller? Why are yuh eyes so blue, and why do yuh talk funny?"

"Talk funny? I can barely understand you. Where do you come from?"

"You can nah understand me, but I can understand you. Whatda you think?"

"Well, I'm glad you can understand me, and maybe someday you can teach me your language."

"Dat's de right answer," Cayman said and then switched to the common language. He had been learning to speak more clearly. "Now, tell me about yourself. Where are you from and why are you on the ship?"

They spent the next hour walking the deck while Cayman explained the workings of the ship. Eventually, Eschon became overloaded with information and asked to sit down. Cayman found some folded canvas for them to sit on.

After they settled in, Cayman leaned forward and said, "Tell me about this island of yours. I only saw it from the ship, but it looked interesting."

Eschon told him about a happy, content life at home and in the village. "But working long, hard days for Lord Creedy could be painful. He liked to use the whip."

"Ya man, I know about dat. Tell me about your village."

Eschon's eyes brightened. No one had ever cared enough to ask him about his life. "Six days a week we work long and hard, but the seventh day we're free. Saturday night, roasting night, is the best. After washing up, a fire pit was dug and filled with wood. Then a pig or lamb would be put on a spit and the roasting began. By sunset a keg of ale and a barrel of wine would be set up in the center of the village for everyone to enjoy. Each family would bring a special dish so that the variety and quantity of food was amazing. My neighbor, Piney, would bring out his mandolin, and his son played fiddle. It was the best five hours of the week."

"It sounds like a wonderful place."

Eschon nodded his head and then told Cayman about Princess Sharman teaching them to read and the Black Storm at Elingale that wiped out the memory of everything she had taught them. He told him about the bat-like creatures, named bohes, attacking their village with fiery breath. And he told him about the spell that recaptured their ability to read and write.

"So, it was magic that taught yuh to read?"

"No. We learned through hard work and study, but it was magical once we knew how to read. I never realized how much I didn't know until I learned to open a book and find the answers."

Over the next two days they ran into each other frequently. They were always learning something new about each other. Cayman even taught Eschon a little of his language.

"If you would say to me, 'don't bother me,' I would say, 'Nuh Baada Me.' If you say, 'Leave me alone,' I say, 'Lef Me.'"

Eschon smiled and said, "Ya man. I'm starting to get it."

Chapter 27

WHEN THEY ARRIVED in the port city of Empeerean, a messenger was waiting for Oden. Oden nodded curtly to the man, jumped onto the back of a waiting horse, and disappeared into the city without saying a word. The messenger then walked over to the Elwin boys and directed them to a wagon.

They bumped along the king's road in the back of a freight wagon loaded with crates and packages being delivered to the palace.

Along the way, Eschon asked, "Did you bring the feather?"

"Gotterslamit! I was in such a hurry to get to the ship that I forgot all about the feather!"

"As obsessed as you are with that feather, it's hard to believe," Eschon said. But before he could say another word, he caught sight of the castle rising from the crest of a hill.

"Ripers! Look at that. I've always thought that Lord Creedy's house was the biggest place I would ever see, but this castle makes his place look like a village hut."

Up ahead, a wide wooden bridge crossed a serpentine river. Two stone lions, resting on marble bases, ceremoniously guarded the bridge. Against a cloudless sky, six blue-tiled turrets rose above the gleaming white walls. Above the arched entrance, banners gently rippled in the breeze.

Thand insisted that the wagon driver drop them off at the castle's main door. Inside the entrance, Eschon inhaled sharply. It seemed too much for him to take in at once. The long corridor in front of them was lined with tall windows on one side and murals of battles on the other. At the end of the entranceway, a white marble staircase ascended twenty feet into the air to meet another long hallway.

Eschon mouthed the words, "I can't believe it."

"Pretty special, huh?" Thand asked his brother. "But if you're here long enough, you'll get used to it. Okay, little brother, now a few quick instructions. After today, never use this front entrance again; it's reserved for special occasions only. Later, I'll show you our door. The hallway on the left goes to the Council Chambers. And on the right is a room for a private audience with the king. If you're lucky, you won't see the inside of either one. Don't ask any more questions. Just follow me. Hurry, I've got to see her."

They ascended the marble steps and turned left down a hall. At the end of the hallway, a soldier stood at ease. When they were about ten feet from him, the guard came to attention and lowered his lance.

"What's this?" asked Eschon as they continued to approach.

Thand turned toward his brother and whispered, "Don't worry. The guards know me."

Thand's eyes narrowed when he didn't recognize the soldier, but he wasn't too worried, yet. In a firm voice, he said, "I'm Thand. I am here to see Princess Sharman."

The guard gave him a steely look, and in a stony voice, he said, "And I am Sydney. Leave this area immediately."

Thand hadn't sailed all the way from Elingale to be turned back at Princess Sharman's door. He took a deep breath, and then exhaled slowly. "She's dying. Let me pass."

The guard glanced down the hall to the primary soldier, looking for an answer. The man shook his head and then called back, "I'm sorry, Thand, Queen's order."

Out of nowhere a voice of authority thundered from behind. "I'm in charge of this patient, not the queen."

Thand and Eschon spun at the same time. Enunciation had just rounded the corner. "Let them pass. My orders."

Thand's eyes widened as his hands dropped to his side. *The wizard!* The tightness in his chest faded at the site of his friend.

Enunciation looked at Eschon, then back to Thand. "Judging by looks, I'd say this must be your brother."

Eschon seemed to have difficulty forming a response. Enunciation patted his shoulder. "We'll talk later."

The young guard swallowed hard and shifted his weight. "I'm not sure," he stammered.

"I'll take responsibility, Sydney. We're all going in."

"Please, sir, keep me out of trouble," Sydney said in a shaky voice. Then he pulled his lance back and stepped to the side.

Thand placed his hand on the door handle and his chest tightened. He tried to visualize a sickly person, but he couldn't picture Princess Sharman any other way than beautiful.

The door opened noiselessly. Orange light flickered from the fireplace and the fragrance of cinnamon hung in the air. A plain, simple chair sat next to a four-poster bed with its lacey curtains tied back. Against the wall was a small table strewn with vials of powders, oils, and white-linen bandages.

Enunciation walked to the princess' side and felt her brow, then motioned the brothers to come forward. Thand's face turned ashen and his eyes teared up. Her skin was pasty-white and her face was gaunt. Her beautiful, long, auburn hair was oily and matted from lack of care. Without thinking, Thand leaned down and kissed her forehead.

"How is she doing?" Eschon whispered.

"As compared to what?" replied Enunciation. "She is obviously sick, but her breathing has become steady. The poison has passed through her system without killing her. But she still hasn't opened her eyes."

Thand picked up the princess' cold hand, placing it against his warm face. He squeezed gently and remembered their parting kiss. His hand twitched, or was it hers? A tear rolled down his face as he kissed her palm. Her lips seemed to part imperceptibly. A faint, questioning syllable was uttered: "Thand?"

Thand grabbed the wizard's arm. "Did you hear that?"

Enunciation spoke her name quietly, but there was no response. He touched her forehead and did a quick examination. Thand thought he saw a slight relaxation in the wizard's facial muscles.

Enunciation looked over his shoulders at Thand and said, "Her pulse has increased a bit, and her breathing is slightly stronger."

Then the wizard gently brushed back her hair and said to Thand, "Kiss her again. I think she's responding to your body warmth."

Thand hesitated. Being this intimate in front of other people didn't seem right.

"Hurry!" Enunciation barked. "Before the queen-bee gets here."

That snapped Thand into action. He leaned over and kissed the princess' lips. They were cool and dry, not soft and warm like during their final kiss on Lapis Lazuli.

The princess stirred, mumbled something, and then slowly opened her eyes for the first time since stepping off the ship. She blinked repeatedly, trying to understand where she was and how she got there. Finally, she focused on Thand and reached for his hand. Then she scowled and, in a weak voice, said, "Why didn't you come sooner?"

At that moment, the door swung open and Queen Twila entered

the room. Her eyes went to Eschon first and then to Thand, who was standing alongside her daughter, holding her hand.

Her face flushed, her eyes glared, and then she snarled. "What is he doing here? Who is this, and why are these Elwin boys here? Guard!"

"Twila, calm down," barked the wizard. "Look at your daughter."

The queen rushed to her side, rudely pushing Thand away.

Enunciation flinched and gave Thand an apologetic look. The wizard looked at the queen and said, "Don't underestimate the power of Thand's presence. He's the first person she has responded to. The boy is the best medicine we can give her right now."

Twila huffed back, "I'm the best medicine for her. I'm her mother. This would've never happened if she hadn't met these boys."

Enunciation's eyes narrowed and he shot back with, "If she hadn't met these boys, she would have drowned in the ocean with Warmund."

Thand's face reddened. He began to speak, but Eschon grabbed his arm and pulled him toward the door.

"Not now," whispered Eschon. "Leave."

Thand jerked away from his brother but reluctantly left. At the end of the hall, he stopped. "Did you hear her? I'm not good enough to be with her daughter."

"Maybe she didn't mean it. She's awful upset right now. It's easy for her to blame you. But think before you talk; you don't want to do anything that will cause her to send you home."

The throbbing in Thand's head began to subside. "Maybe you're right. For the sake of the princess, I'll try to forget it."

They walked toward the staircase. Then, at the first step, Thand stopped and turned toward his brother. In a scathing voice, he said, "But I can't forget this. That woman has never liked me. My lack of education and money makes me inferior in her mind. I guess my ears and short height add to her dislike. But I'll show her how inferior I am once I have the Kookachoo Feather back in my hand."

Chapter 28

*T*HAND WAS AT ease with himself for the first time since finding the feather. It was like the first weeks on Lapis Lazuli, when every minute with the princess seemed to be happy. He wanted to believe that he had made a difference in Princess Sharman's recovery, but he knew that Enunciation's herbs and oils had played a bigger role. A pink, two-inch scar at the base of her neck was the only visible sign of the trauma. When asked what she remembered, she only recalled seeing all of the pomp and ceremony and then starting down the gangplank. The next thing that she recalled was a warm hand on her cheek.

They strolled through the formal gardens to an opening in the tall, cropped hedge where a stone bench sat in recess. The view was pastoral. A perfectly manicured lawn sloped down to a small, mirror-like lake dappled with ducks and swans. Princess Sharman gave details of their search for her uncle and the encounter with Skull Island. She asked if he had met Cayman.

"Do you mean the dark-skinned sailor?" Thand answered indifferently. "Only briefly."

"You should take time and talk to him. He's a very interesting man."

"I'll leave him to Eschon. They're buddies."

Thand knew it was the perfect moment to tell her about the Kookachoo Bird's feather and refocus her thoughts on them. But he wasn't sure how much to reveal since he still hadn't mastered its use. Instead, he talked about how helpless he had felt upon learning of the assassination attempt.

"If I ever find out who's responsible for this, I'm going to destroy them."

The princess laughed. "What are you going to do? Kill him with kindness?"

Thand winced. "Ouch. But you're right. I have no fighting skills."

"Nor do I. I've always had someone assigned to protect me."

"Yeah, that really worked well when you were getting off the ship," he said sarcastically. "We need to be able to take care of ourselves."

"I agree. I'm tired of being treated like a little girl."

Their eyes met and they nodded. The time had come to learn self-defense and become skilled at protecting themselves.

Sharman punched Thand in the arm playfully. "I'll talk to my father. I'm sure he'll agree. Now, enough of this. Tell me about Elingale. What has changed since I've left?"

Thand looked down and hesitated. *Tell her.* "Not much."

"Really? With the Elwins in charge of the land and Lord Creedy in jail, nothing's changed?"

"Well, yes. We are spending a lot of time learning to operate the new farm equipment your father sent. And of course the school is doing well, but nothing really exciting."

"Then maybe I need to go back and stir things up," she laughed.

"Ripers! That would be great. You and I back on Lapis Lazuli."

Chapter 29

Baylock stepped outside of the Cranium for the first time in several days. Immediately, he felt the low level of energy surrounding the island. He had been so distracted with his work that he had forgotten to recharge it. In fact, it was so low that anyone could have stumbled onto the island unnoticed. He used his usual chant, but the power needed to restore the shield left him light-headed. He chided himself for the dangerous lapse. If an enemy attacked right now, he would break through his first line of defense.

The wizard hurried inside and gave Sedgley orders to go out and search the island for intruders. Sedgley let out a bark of laughter. "Me? Why not you? It's your island."

"Stop questioning me, Sedgley. Do as you're told," Baylock replied in a mildly threatening voice.

"But it's dangerous out there. What about all those monstrous creatures?"

"It's daylight and you know what to avoid. If you use that brain for more than just challenging my orders, you won't have any trouble. Now, go. Before I make you a meal for my pets."

Baylock escorted Sedgley to the observation platform to make sure that his order was carried out. Sedgley stepped off the platform and looked back at Baylock as if hoping he could change his mind. The wizard bore into him with his yellow, wolf-like eyes. Sedgley turned away immediately, his face ashen white. Then, speaking over his shoulder quietly, he said, "Yes, Your Wizardship, leaving right now. Is there anything I can pick up for you while I'm out?"

Baylock heard him grumble but was satisfied that he was going to do as ordered.

About an hour later, Sedgley walked into the Cranium prodding an emaciated man with a stick.

"Behold, see what I found, Your Wizardship. Look at this poor creature. He was lying on the beach, asking for food and water. How could I say no?"

"You fool! Take him outside. Give him something to drink if you must and then come back at once."

Sedgley gave Baylock a sidelong glance but took the man outside. When Sedgley returned he said, "Done as ordered."

Baylock's nostrils flared. "You idiot, now he's seen our fortress. If he goes back home and tells people what's here, then other men will follow. I won't allow that to happen."

"I'll have a talk with him and impress on him how important it is to forget what he's seen. We'll drop him off the next time we go to Whistlers Key."

Baylock swept his arm toward the entrance angrily. "You're a bigger fool than I thought. Go out and tie his hands and feet. If he escapes, you're dinner for Mactabilis."

Baylock sighed heavily and returned to his laboratory to continue his work. He began tinkering with the formula that had left the young boy on Raintree Island mute. It had been partially successful in that the boy couldn't say the word *useless*, but he had no desire to rule a world of mute people.

The following day, Baylock had the stranger brought to the laboratory. The man was panting hard from the exertion of climbing three stories. Baylock asked himself if experimenting on someone so weak was worth it. His concern was not for the man's health, but for wasting his precious elements. *Live test subjects are rare. Use him.*

He asked the stranger to tell him a little bit about himself to establish that he was articulate. In midsentence, Baylock chanted a few words. From emptiness, fog appeared, and when it lifted, the man was covered with a light gray powder. He choked but continued telling his story.

"Good, so far," said Baylock. "Now, do as I command. Say the word *no*."

The man said *yes*. Sedgley gave Baylock a worried stare.

Baylock told the confused man to say *yes*, but the word *no* came out. Then Baylock repeated the experiment on the visibly shaken man and got the same results.

"Sedgley, return the man to the observation platform and double his allotment of food and water. But keep his one leg shackled. I'm not through with him."

Chapter 30

THAND WAS STARING out the window and thinking about the stinging words of Queen Twila. When an errand runner tapped him on the shoulder, he jumped. The boy handed him a message and left in a hurry. Thand wasted no time opening the note. It read, "Defensive training will begin in the morning at eight. Be on time and ready for a challenging day."

He rubbed the back of his neck. "So soon?"

The next morning, Thand woke up with a flutter in his stomach. He wanted to stay in bed, not learn to fight. Talking about self-defense was easy; doing something about it was not. *Maybe Eschon would go in my place.* Then he remembered that his brother was spending all of his time with Enunciation. Dismissing his cowardly thoughts, he dressed and went to the ring.

He showed up in brown wool slacks and a bloused green shirt. A piece of rope held up his pants. This was his first time in the arena, and he was nervous. A few long moments passed, and then the princess entered the arena. She was wearing black leather pants, a scoop-neck blouse, and a wide leather belt around her waist. Her hair was tied back with a yellow silk band. The men in the training area stopped and watched her enter.

Thand couldn't believe his eyes. *Why is she dressed like that? Aren't we going to be down in the dirt, wrestling with the instructor, hitting and kicking? Maybe today is just oral instruction. Still, those clothes are too flashy.*

The practice area was enclosed on three sides by a ten-foot stone wall. Within the training space were archery targets and several hacked-up wooden posts used for practicing sword strikes. Cayman stood near a straw-stuffed man that was hanging from a pillar. He pulled on a strand of his red dreadlocks and strode over to the princess. He was dressed in black and walked with his shoulders back and chin held high, perfect posture. A confident smile played across his face.

Thand clenched his jaw. *What's he doing here? I thought Oden would train us.*

They had met briefly on the ship, but Thand thought he was just a low-ranking sailor.

Cayman planted a light kiss on both cheeks of the princess, then walked over to Thand and introduced himself. When he put out his hand to shake, Thand ignored him.

Cayman didn't seem to take offense and didn't waste any time with pleasantries.

"Both of you hold your arms straight out and make a fist."

Cayman took Thand's arm and gripped his forearm, bicep, and shoulder.

"Not bad. Your arms are strong, but you are muscle-bound. You'll need to work on flexibility."

Cayman went through the same process with Princess Sharman. Thand's eyes narrowed. He thought Cayman was spending too much time exploring her shoulder.

Cayman stepped back from her and said, "You can't train. That wound in your right shoulder hasn't healed enough. Vigorous training could reopen it."

"Then it's a good thing that I'm left handed," she said with a cocky smile.

He shrugged, and then squeezed her back, waist, and hips.

"You'll have to build your upper body strength."

Thand's face turned red. "You seem to enjoy the evaluation part a little too much."

Cayman laughed. "You're next."

The morning was mostly used for stretching and building muscle tone. During a break, Cayman grabbed his own sword and pointed out the basic parts of the sword. Pommel, guard, and point were all that Thand could remember.

"We don't want to lose any hands or arms today, so we will train with a heavy wooden sword."

In the afternoon they practiced using single-handed and two-handed grips. And just when they thought the day was over, Cayman made them go through footwork and stepping exercises.

At the end of the practice session, Thand threw down his wooden sword and removed his protective padding. The first day of training was over, and every muscle in his body hurt. Cayman helped the princess remove her padding and then returned her sword to the training box.

Thand mumbled something unkind under his breath, and Cayman gave him a hard look. "Tomorrow will be worse."

Chapter 31

SCHON SAT AT the dining table with Thand and Princess Sharman. They were just three of King Treutlen's dozen invited guests. Tonight's banquet was small and informal compared to a dignitary reception, but the king wanted to celebrate his daughter's recovery. Lucky for all, the king was not a windy speaker and kept the evening low-key.

This was Eschon's first time in the Banquet Hall. Surveying the room, he leaned in and said, "This place is so big that it could entertain the entire population of Elingale."

The princess clapped her hands. "Oh, wouldn't that be fun. I'd love to do that. If only we could find a way to get everyone here."

The delicate smell of roasted almonds floated on the air, hinting at what was to come. Eschon turned toward the princess and asked, "What wonderful concoction have your chefs come up with for tonight?"

"See for yourself," said the princess, as a dozen servants walked into the room carrying heavy, silver platters on their shoulders.

The head chef cleared his throat in order to get everyone's attention. "Tonight, a custard-like dish called *blancmange* will be served. The tasty dish consists of a paste of chicken blended with rice, boiled in almond milk, seasoned with sugar, salt, and ginger, and then cooked until very thick. It is garnished with fried almonds and anise."

The food was set in front of the diners, still covered. When the king nodded to the head chef, all the plates were uncovered at the same time.

"Pretty impressive," said Eschon. "But it's flavor that counts, not the ceremony." He tasted the food and smiled. "Next trip we bring Mother. If she could learn to cook like this, I'd never leave home."

In between bites of food, Princess Sharman and Thand took turns complaining about the exhausting day of training. A sling, cradling the princess' right arm, underscored the level of physical activity.

Thand leaned sideways and touched his shoulder to the princess. "Why don't you rest up tomorrow? I'll go to training by myself."

"What, and show Cayman I can't keep up? No. I'll be there."

Thand stood and then raised his pant leg. "Look, brother. Every one of these bruises was caused by Cayman. He uses his practice sword like a club. A light tap would have been sufficient, but he seemed to enjoy making welts appear."

Eschon rolled his eyes. He wasn't interested in listening to Thand play the victim. Other than the first day on the ship, his brother had virtually ignored him. If he hadn't met Cayman and Enunciation, he would have gone crazy with boredom.

He forced what he thought might be a sympathetic smile. Then he turned to the princess and chatted about the wonderful things that Enunciation was teaching him. She seemed interested in listening, so he told her that he felt a powerful calling to become part of the magical life of wizardry.

Thand cut into their conversation. "So, Enunciation has been entertaining you with common tricks."

Eschon's eyes narrowed. *I thought those two were friends.* "No, Thand. That's not what real magicians do," he said in a sharp voice. "I've learned a lot from the wizard, and I'm seriously thinking about becoming an apprentice. I want to learn how to craft objects and cast spells that would help the people of Elingale."

Thand wrinkled his nose. "You're just dazzled by all of the new experiences. It'll pass."

Eschon just shook his head and sighed. *He's become so self-centered that there's no sense in trying to explain how I feel.*

While the princess was busy speaking to someone else, Thand leaned close to his brother so no one could hear. "Don't worry about learning wizardry. With the power of my feather, we won't need magic."

Eschon's nostrils flared. "No, Thand. This is something I want to do for myself. I want to become self-reliant, and you're not going to stop me."

"All right, relax. But it seems like a waste of time. I would think that you'd want to help me rule."

"Rule! Do you hear yourself? What happened to using the power to help others and improve life in Elingale?"

Thand shifted in his chair, glanced around the table, and then turned back. "Keep your voice down. We can talk about this later."

So, he hasn't told the princess about the feather.

Eschon looked hard at his brother, then in a clear voice asked, "Why always later, Thand? When do you plan on telling her?"

Thand's eyes grew big. He put his index finger to his lips in a gesture to stop Eschon from talking, but Eschon's patience with his brother was nearing its limit. "Or should I do it for you?"

Thand's body stiffened and he shot a quick glance at the

princess, who was still engaged with a guest. "We agreed to keep this a secret until I said it was okay."

Eschon stood up. *Enough.* He looked straight into Thand's eyes. "Tell me something, oh wise brother. Do people in love keep secrets or share them?"

Chapter 32

CAYMAN LOWERED HIS eyes as he spoke to King Treutlen. "Yes, Your Majesty, it's true that I was raised by thieves, cutthroats, and murderers. It's correct to call them pirates."

Oden stepped up alongside Cayman. "Your Grace, with permission."

The king looked down from his chair, his mood was unreadable. "Go on."

"When I first met this man, I didn't like him."

Cayman's shoulders dropped noticeably.

"My initial impression was wrong. As I told you earlier, his unselfish action saved my life. And Cayman's eagerness to assimilate won over the crew in less than a week. He's made an honest effort to shed his past. I say he's trustworthy."

The king questioned Cayman for thirty minutes before he was satisfied. Then a handshake from the king welcomed him into his service.

A discussion regarding the assassin's motivation followed. Princess Sharman had no known enemies, but the king had many. After some discussion, it was agreed that revenge was the most likely motive. Working from that point of view, Cayman was to proceed to Empeerean and start asking questions.

Not wanting to waste time, Cayman left the meeting and walked to the stables. He had a spring in his step. For most of his adult life, trust had been a missing feature. No one placed confidence in a pirate. But that had just changed. King Treutlen had entrusted him with the task of finding the assassin. And of all people, Oden had recommended him. But as he entered the stable, his steps became heavier. Responsibility could be a considerable burden.

Cayman was aware that precious days had slipped away while the palace was consumed with the health of the princess. Hopefully, the lack of a retaliatory response had lulled the assassin into thinking that he got away with murder.

He climbed on his horse and clopped over the wooden bridge. His plan was to visit the area around the docks and put himself in the mind of the killer. When he turned onto the main road, he gave the horse a nudge. The steed leaped forward, showing off his speed. For ten exhilarating minutes they sped through the broadleaf forest and past lush fields of grain. At the crest of a steep hill, he paused to rest the horse.

Empeerean was visible in the hazy distance. The port city, he learned, had grown to about seven thousand people. Every major merchant, from shoemakers to booksellers, had a business establishment that sold goods to anyone who had coin. The capital city even boasted ten taverns and five inns.

At the city limits, Cayman pulled the horse back to a canter. Pedestrian traffic was heavy, and racing through the streets was against the law. He turned a corner and headed for the docks.

"Hey mon," he heard as a fellow sailor gave him a wave. Some phrases of his laidback speech were catching on.

At the waterfront he made his way to Timme's Tavern House. It was the nearest building to the dock with enough height to allow a straight shot at the ship. He tied-off his horse and studied the area. The distance from the rooftop to the gangplank looked to be about three hundred yards. The average effective range of a good bow was two hundred to two hundred and fifty yards. That meant the arrow must have been shot by a modified crossbow.

He entered the establishment. Hazy tobacco smoke filled the tavern room. Serving girls wove between customers, avoiding groping hands, while never spilling a drop. A cacophony of sounds made shouting necessary.

Scanning the room, he found the owner. Timme was a short, barrel-chested man with a moon face. Snow-white hair matched his spotless apron. Cayman introduced himself and began asking questions. The keeper's eyes darted around the room. He wasn't ignoring Cayman. He had trained himself to listen and watch at the same time. Knowing the difference between a tipsy customer and a troublemaker was imperative to survive in this type of business.

Timme shouted to Cayman: "They're a hungry lot today."

"And have a lot to say."

"How is Princess Sharman?" asked the barkeep. "I hear it's very serious."

Hoping to prevent a second attempt on her life, Cayman shook his head. "Yes, she's critically ill. We don't expect her to make it. That's why I need your help."

His shoulders slumped. "We were hoping it was just a rumor."

"If you help," Cayman said, "we can bring the son-of-ashade to justice."

Timme directed Cayman to a young, petite girl who he said was his wife. Cayman seemed doubtful, but crossed the room, and then introduced himself. During the interview, the wife explained that she had been out in the kitchen house and overheard two men talking about arrows and wind. They were on the other side of a rear fence, and she only saw the tops of their heads. One wore a green felt archer's hat, and the other had coal-black hair. That was all she knew.

While Cayman would have liked to have more information, especially facial features, at least he learned that the shooter had an accomplice. Knowing the fence height, he added two more inches and came up with five feet, two inches tall.

When Cayman came back inside, Timme pointed to a fidgety, middle-aged woman in a rumpled dress who was standing near the rear exit. "She came to me when you were talking with the wife. She claims she knows the killer. I told her you'd talk to her."

He walked up to the mousy woman, smiled, and introduced himself. She took a step back and frowned. "Who are you?" she said in a shrill voice. "Where's Cayman? They told me to talk to him."

"I am Cayman. What can you tell me?"

Her head flinched back. "Oh, I thought you'd look…different."

Cayman ignored the insinuation.

"Okay, I guess it's all right. I saw Warmund on the day of the shooting. He had a long cape over his shoulders. 'Why would someone wear that on a hot day?' I asked myself. I'll tell you why. He had a bow hidden under it."

Cayman was already skeptical. The day had been cool. "And how do you know what Warmund looks like?"

"Wh-why, we were close friends. When we were young'uns," she said with a wink.

"But you're ten years older than him. How's that possible?"

Her forehead wrinkled. "My personal life is none of your business."

"So, why did he want to kill his own niece?"

"What kind of investigator are you? He'd gone mad while

drifting in the hot sun for all that time. Warmund blamed the princess for his hardship and wanted her dead. Can't you figure out anything?"

Cayman suppressed a laugh. "Where's Warmund now?"

She tilted her head to the side and stared at him like he had two heads. "What? How am I to know? You're the detective. You find him."

Cayman patted the lady on the back and nudged her toward the door. "Thank you for all your help."

But halfway out the door she turned and called in a twittering voice, "I want my reward money when he's found. I won't be cheated."

Timme came over and set a beer in front of him. "She's a little daft. Here, thought you might like this."

Cayman chuckled and nodded his thanks. Lifting the tankard, he took a sip. His eyes scrunched up. Now he understood why the beer was free.

Chapter 33

THAND WALKED TO the training arena grinding his teeth. *That jolthead brother of mine! He's forcing my hand.* At breakfast, Eschon had made a second veiled threat to tell Princess Sharman about the Kookachoo Bird feather if Thand didn't do it soon.

Princess Sharman was already on the practice field when Thand joined her. A substitute instructor was there to greet them. They were told Cayman was in the city and would not coach them today. Thand thought training that day was vigorous, but that the session went well. No aggravation from Cayman made time fly by.

After removing their equipment, Thand asked the princess, "Is there anywhere we can meet tonight? I have something important to tell you."

"This sounds so romantic," she said with a gleam in her eye. "The library is usually quiet in the evening. I'll meet you there after dinner."

That evening they met in the hall and entered the library together. Thand looked around, making sure they were alone. He guided the princess to a secluded spot, then lifted a section of hair from her shoulder and inspected the neck wound. A mischievous smile crossed his face. Mocking Cayman, he squeezed her shoulders, waist, and hip.

From the entrance door of the library, they heard an "ahem." Thand dropped his hands immediately and turned, red-faced, toward the sound.

"Nanny Laila," the princess said. "It's nice to see you. What do you want?"

A flush crept across the nanny's cheeks as she walked toward the couple. Laila had been the governess for the princess since her birth. "The queen has ordered me to keep you company this evening."

Indignation flashed across the princess' face. She took a deep breath, then resumed a pleasant smile. In a conspiratorial voice, she said, "I know what my mother really wants, and I also know I can trust you. Please, just sit near the door and read a book. Pay no attention to anything you hear or see. That way you'll be able to report that it was a quiet evening."

Nanny Laila smiled and gave a knowing nod. "That's just what I would have suggested."

Thand grabbed a chair, then set it near the door. He leaned down to the nanny and whispered his thanks. They hurried to the opposite end of the great room and found a nook with two chairs.

The princess leaned forward and grabbed Thand's arm. "Now, what's the secret?"

Thand scratched the back of his hand. "Do you remember the Kookachoo Bird legend?"

Princess Sharman sat up straight. "Yes."

"A few days after you left, I found a large white feather lying on the trail to the beach. It was in plain sight, like I was supposed to find it." He paused for dramatic effect and then blurted out, "It's the Kookachoo Bird's tail feather!"

"No. You're kidding! I thought that it was just a legend. How can you be sure?"

"Just believe me. It's the real thing."

"What are you going to do with it? Do you have it with you? I'd love to see it."

"No. It is hidden in my house. No one knows except Eschon, but I don't know if I can trust him anymore."

The princess frowned. "Eschon is your brother. Why wouldn't you trust him?"

"He wants it for himself, but it's mine. I'm the one who found it. I know its power can twist a person's thinking. That's why his behavior has been so strange."

"Twisted thinking? What's wrong with his behavior? Thand, this doesn't sound like you. Are you all right? Why are you so secretive about this? Ordinarily, you would have shared this good news with everyone." Her face tightened. "You are going to share this with everyone, right?"

"Of course."

Princess Sharman hesitated, then continued. "Have any of the things from the legend come to pass?"

"I was all set to use it when Oden came ashore and told me about your injury. I couldn't think of anything but you. I came here as fast as possible and left the feather behind."

"That's very sweet. I'm flattered. But why didn't you tell me earlier when I asked for news?"

Thand looked down and became unnaturally quiet, then swallowed hard. "I was going to tell you sooner, but it never seemed to be the right time."

She crossed her arms. "How about all the time we spent together while I was recuperating," she said in a rising voice. "You couldn't find time to tell me then?"

He shook his head slightly and stammered, "I didn't think you needed to know. I mean, at that time you didn't. But that was before. Now I do."

Princess Sharman adopted a challenging tone. "So, you don't trust me either."

"No, no. I'm telling you right now; that shows I trust you."

She looked him in the eye and dropped her arms. "Maybe you only trust me when it's convenient. I'm hurt. I thought our relationship was stronger than this."

"I'm sorry. I didn't think it was that important."

"Important! When isn't trust important? And if the legend is true, it will be the most important thing that ever happened in your life. And you waited till now to tell me?"

"But—"

"This is what Eschon was talking about this morning," the princess said in a soft voice. Then she stood, turned her back on Thand, and moved toward the door. "Laila, it's time I retire."

Thand grabbed her arm but she pulled away. He yelled, "I'm sorry" to the retreating princess. Laila put her arm around the princess' waist, looked back, and gave Thand a withering look.

He left the library and walked to his room with his arms hanging slack at his side. Once there, he collapsed onto the bed. He covered his eyes with an arm and sighed heavily. *What's happening? Why can't anyone see what I see?*

A few minutes later, Eschon walked in, humming a tune. He stopped in his tracks. "I thought you'd be with the princess."

Thand didn't want to talk about her, so instead he asked, "What do you think of Adrianna Island? Are you glad you came?"

Eschon relaxed. He thanked his brother for letting him come

along. Every minute seemed to be a new experience. Enunciation was the most incredible man he had ever met.

After a few minutes of excited talk, Thand raised a hand to his brother's face. "Enough about you. I have something more important to talk about."

Eschon looked offended. "I don't want to talk about your feather."

"It's not about the feather; it's about Princess Sharman. She got angry with me and walked away."

Eschon's eyes narrowed. "So, it is about the feather."

"Her feelings were hurt. She wanted to know why I didn't tell her sooner. She said I didn't trust her. But if she would just hear me out, I could tell her that I'm going to build her a castle on Lapis Lazuli."

Eschon's mouth fell open. "What did you say? A castle!"

"Don't worry. It'll be big enough for you and Mother to live in. It will also be big enough to make Queen Twila jealous."

"What? I don't want to live in a castle. And I doubt that Mother does either. Queen Twila? Who cares?"

Thand was staring at the ceiling, looking like he hadn't heard a word his brother spoke. "I'll be able to give her everything, much more than she has now. She won't miss any of this."

Eschon's eyes turned cold. "What about your ideas for a better school, buying new medicines, and improving living conditions?"

"Oh, those. I'm still going to do that, just later."

"Thand, I've never heard you sound so selfish."

He looked at Eschon as if seeing him for the first time. "Now I see what you're worried about. You think I won't share my new wealth with you."

"Kin! What's wrong with you? You sound like you're possessed by a greed demon."

Thand's face reddened. "Why shouldn't I get all the things I want? After all the sacrifices I've made for Elingale. It was I who saved the princess from drowning. I endured Lord Creedy's whip. I, not you, nearly died from the incurro-wolf bite. And it was I who led the revolt against Creedy. I deserve it."

Eschon's voice was dripping with bitterness. "And you did this all by yourself, without any help from us. Our hero."

"The feather was left for me. I decide how to use the power. It will give me whatever I want. And right now, I want Princess Sharman to be happy and love me. If that means I have to build a castle on Lapis Lazuli, I will."

Eschon shook his head. "You don't even know how to use the feather. Besides, what makes you think the princess wants you to do this? Who said she doesn't love you?"

"You saw the way Queen Twila treated me, as if I wasn't good enough for her daughter. And Oden and Cayman are showing too much interest in her. If I could give her more than anyone else, she would stay with me forever."

"Thand, I'm your brother, and I love you. Please listen to me. Princess Sharman, I, Mother, and all of the Elwins don't care about your riches. We'd rather have the kind, thoughtful, and funny Thand back. When we get home, throw that feather away."

"Yeah, so you can take it! Get out of here. Run to your new father, Enunciation. I don't need you anymore."

Chapter 34

AFTER THE QUARREL with Thand, Eschon avoided his brother as much as possible.

Today he was going to spend the day at the king's library. In order to impress Enunciation, he needed to improve his reading skills. He found the massive room in a separate wing of the castle. The minute he walked in, he could feel magic. He was expecting a dark room lit by many candles, but instead the library shone like it was midday. He looked to the ceilings and saw dozens of rectangles mounted in the ceiling, emitting a yellow-white light that matched the noonday sun. He had never seen anything so wondrous.

The walls were paneled in a light-colored wood, and the floors were black marble. Stone columns supported a second-story balcony that housed thousands of books. *What a beautiful place. No wonder Princess Sharman is so smart.* He spun in a slow circle, eyebrows squishing together, wondering where to begin.

At the head of the stairs he saw a sign that read *Simplex Carminibus*, meaning simple spells. "That's where I'll start," he said to no one.

As he browsed among the stacks, he found a bright red book etched in gold with the title *Elemental Sorcery.* He removed it from the shelf, then sat at a nearby table. Ancient symbols and lists of elements filled the beginning pages. Not understanding most of them, he moved to the next section, where he found instructions for making a protective charm. The directions: "In a small cloth bag insert garlic, red peppers, marjoram, and rose petals. Tie the bag with a leather cord and then touch it with a magical wand and repeat:

> *"Air cannot harm me.*
> *Fire cannot burn me.*
> *Water cannot drown me.*
> *Earth cannot entomb me."*

Then hang the bag around the neck to prevent injury or harm.

He wrote down the ingredients, and after several more hours in the library, he headed for the kitchen to search for the ingredients.

That night, he arrived for dinner wearing a small packet around his neck. The rose petals did little to offset the smell of garlic. A few minutes later, Enunciation walked into the room and wrinkled his nose. He walked over to Eschon, then whispered, "I'll teach you an improved version later."

"Is that why no one will sit next to me?"

The wizard showed a wide grin and nodded.

After the evening meal, the magician and his apprentice retired to the study. The wizard asked for news about Elingale. After a quick update, Eschon told the story of the grotto bone.

"At first we thought it was a rock, and then we thought it was a boulder. But when it was fully uncovered, we didn't know what to think. It was Thand who figured it out—a dragon bone!"

Enunciation clapped his hands and leaned forward. "This is

wonderful! A source for dragon-bone powder. It's an extremely powerful component in magic—very rare and hard to find. If we only knew where dragons go to die…Hey, do you think the Elwins would sell me a section of the bone?"

"No. But we'll give you as much as you want. Without your help, we wouldn't have defeated Baylock's spell. "

Eschon had wanted to tell Enunciation the story of the Kookachoo feather and get his opinion. Was it the power of the feather or Thand himself causing this radical change in his personality? But before the topic came up, the evening was abruptly concluded when a sharp pain contorted the wizard's face.

He pressed his hand to his chest and said, "We'll talk tomorrow. Right now, I need some rest."

Eschon was unsure if leaving the wizard alone was a good idea. But knowing no solution, he respected Enunciation's wishes and walked back to his room, half expecting to hear someone call for the physician.

His castle bedchamber was triple the size of his own bedroom at home. There were three separate pieces of furniture just for clothes. One was a sea chest; another had five rows of drawers. The third piece was called an armoire. *Who possessed that many clothes?*

His bed was so wide that he could easily share it with two other people. All of this space just for him. It made no sense, but this night he was happy to have the privacy. A great deal was on his mind.

Time had seemed to speed up since leaving Lapis Lazuli. The world had grown larger, and a new adventure lay around every corner. He had to make a decision, but surprisingly, returning home wasn't a part of it. Enunciation had inspired him and sparked a new passion. It wasn't just the curiosity of magic or the magnetism of Enunciation's personality. This new awareness was more intense. It was like the spirit of the earth was calling him to become a member of wizardry. He got goose bumps whenever he thought about learning magic.

Divergence. It was a word he had just learned. The dictionary said it meant to branch off, extend in a different direction. That's what would happen today if Enunciation gave him the right answer.

At this time of day, the wizard was usually alone in his research room. Eschon dressed quickly and snaked through the hallways, rehearsing his speech several times. He paused at the carved oak doors and took a deep breath. Without further hesitation, he pulled on the door.

The wizard was sitting in a nearby chair with his head buried in a book. Usually Eschon wouldn't have disturbed him, but this was too important. He cleared his throat.

"Are you feeling better? If so, I'd like to talk to you."

Enunciation pointed to a nearby chair, then closed the book. He pushed up his glasses and said, "What can I do for you today, my friend?"

Again, Eschon cleared his throat and then, in a strong voice, he spoke. "I don't know how to say this, but I feel like the spirit of earth is calling me, telling me to take up the art of magic. I feel like I'm destined to become a wizard, and I would like you to be my teacher."

Enunciation smiled. "I'm not surprised. I felt your attraction for the art when we first shook hands. I'm pleased that you're following your instinct. You're correct; it is a calling, but a very special calling. Learning the ways of wizardry can give you great power, the ability to control your life and thereby affect the lives of others. But it is a skill that comes with great responsibility."

Eschon nodded vigorously.

"Some come to magic in hopes of wielding power over others, to force them to act against their own will. Others come to learn, to create, and to build for the good of the community."

The would-be apprentice sat rigid, his hands folded, uncertain if this was a lecture or the beginning of an approval.

"I will only tutor you if you commit to using magic for the good of your fellow man."

Eschon's eyes lit up as an uncontainable smile spread across his face.

"But you must understand that a wizard's life is solitary. It is a life devoted to study and research. There is little time for anything else. A wizard makes a poor husband or father. He lacks the proper amount of time to do either job correctly. However, without those distractions, he can put the welfare of the community above all else. You must understand this before you make a choice. Are you prepared for this way of life?"

This was a profound decision for someone who was an illiterate farm boy until recently. *Can I really do this?*

"I can't say that I am or that I'm not. I've never known this type of living. But I can say that I'll be faithful to honorable achievement through the science of magic."

Enunciation seemed surprised by his choice of words. "Already, you speak like a wizard. And now that I know you're committed, I'll arrange for you to meet the most awesome creature on earth."

Chapter 35

CAYMAN CAME BACK to Empeerean City to revisit Timme's Tavern. This was the largest city that he had ever seen, so he took a ride down to the market square. The area was paved in cobblestones to prevent the buildup of ruts that plagued the dirt roads of most towns. It had the additional advantage of keeping the area free from mud or dust. Open tents and wooden carts were filled with every need one could want. A clock on a wooden tower stood in the center of the square. The side streets leading to the main square were lined with merchants such as bakers, spice merchants, ropemakers, chandlers, and tavern-keepers. There wasn't a need that couldn't be satisfied here.

Cayman circled back, tied his horse behind the tavern, and came in through a side door. He had just ordered a tanker of ale when, from behind him, he heard someone clear his throat. He turned around to see Oden.

"Order the mead unless you like sour beer," suggested Cayman.

"I've noticed that your accent is starting to disappear."

"I'm trying to fit in. Don't yuh know?"

Oden smiled and called for the wine, then leaned in close so as not to be overheard. "I've been thinking about possible suspects. There was a trusted ally, The Duke of Glyndon, who had extensive holdings along the Aerie River. It's the one that runs along the base of the mountain that holds Enunciation's castle. In his craving for power, he led a rebellion and declared himself king of all lands west of the mountains. That was treason, which of course led to a brutal war. After King Treutlen regained control of the area, he exiled the duke to a prison island and offered amnesty to his soldiers if they'd pledge their allegiance. To save their skins, they took the offer, but some soldiers have remained treasonous."

Cayman nodded. "And one of the double-crossers got hold of a crossbow and tried to get even with the king by killing his only daughter."

"Yes," Oden agreed. "Or it could be a nobleman who had lost power in the struggle for the west, or someone who had been promised a duchy in Glyndon's court if the rebellion had been successful."

Cayman leaned back in his chair. "That's a lot of possibilities."

"There are too many former soldiers for you to interview, so I'll send out a few other men to see what they can uncover. I'll try to find out who the major losers were and interrogate them myself. Where are you going from here?"

"I plan to talk with Creedy next, but is there anyone else I should investigate?"

Oden looked at the ceiling and rubbed the back of his neck. "The Wizard Baylock is a long shot but must be considered. He's a self-serving, vindictive man who was outsmarted by Thand and Princess Sharman. He also holds a grudge against the king. Unfortunately, he escaped. We don't even know where to look."

Chapter 36

AFTER MEETING WITH Enunciation, Eschon returned to his room. But he barely slept that night trying to figure out what the most awesome creature on earth could be. Lapis Lazuli was a simple island, and the most awesome creature he could think of was a mountain lion. A gigantic bear would be fearsome, too. But maybe Enunciation had meant something mythical, like a unicorn.

Morning finally arrived and Eschon bounded out of bed, dressed, and then hurried to the stable, where Oden was calmly waiting.

"Where are the horses? Is Cayman coming?" Eschon asked anxiously. But before Oden could answer, Thand and Princess Sharman arrived at the barn door, looking like they were still asleep.

"Good. Now all we need is the other wizard," Oden said.

"I thought he'd be here," Eschon said, while looking toward the castle. "Other?"

"Am I not speaking with one now?" Oden asked, seeming to know the answer.

Eschon looked around and then realized the meaning of the question. Suddenly, he felt taller. His chest thrust out. "I am or will be. I mean, I hope so."

Oden put his hand on Eschon's shoulder. "The time for doubting is over. In a moment, you will meet a creature from the aboriginal time, a direct descendent of the earliest and greatest dragon ever to live, Slaythemaû the First."

Princess Sharman burst out laughing. "Not that again! Dragons? And Eschon a wizard? Maybe I still have a fever. Please, tell me, what game are we playing?"

Oden sighed heavily. "This is no game, Princess, and its past time you learn about dragons. Despite all the previous denials you've heard, they really do exist and have since the recording of history. Their numbers have drastically decreased because man destroys what he cannot control. They have been hunted and driven into seclusion, but dragons have survived."

The princess shrugged and shook her head. "Men and their monsters, it never ends."

They should've brought Cayman and left her back at the castle, Eschon thought.

"Pay attention," Oden commanded in a strong voice. "It's important that everyone do exactly as I say when we get to the cave. This dragon is dangerous and unpredictable. Now, follow me and your questions will be answered."

Eschon walked beside Oden, his arms swinging like a parade soldier. He could hardly wait to see what this was all about.

They walked along a switchback trail that led up into the hillside. It had rained the night before, so they dodged puddles as they went. The trail quickly grew steep. At the midway point, they stopped to catch their breath. Oden pointed to a rocky overhang three hundred feet ahead. It was to be their destination. Already, they could smell a strange odor like burnt trees mixed with charred meat.

Within a short period of time, they were on top of a flat, rocky ledge. The unusual odor grew stronger. Just ahead and to the right was the entrance to a large cave. Scorched rocks and bones littered the area. They were about fifty feet from the entrance when a deep rumbling sound, like a sleeping giant awakening, reverberated from inside the cave.

Princess Sharman stopped suddenly and gripped Thand's arm. Thand flinched and swallowed hard. Eschon's senses went to high alert.

Is this really happening? Eschon thought. The myths and fables must be true. The rumors and sightings were not just someone's wild imagination.

He thought back to the meetinghouse in Elingale, with evening fires filled with stories of lore. He recalled the tale of a young boy risking his life to get to an inaccessible island where a golden dragon egg rested. The story said the boy took the egg and nursed it until it hatched. When the grateful young dragon was strong enough, it flew the boy to a lair filled with riches. Many said that the story was untrue. The boy died on the island, and his bones were still in the cave. No one knew for sure, but Eschon had always believed the boy and dragon were still alive, living a magical life.

The rumbling sound from the cave stopped. Then, without warning, an orange flame blasted past the opening, barely missing the group.

Oden stretched out his arm in a stopping motion. "Her power of smell is very strong. She knows something is out here and has sent a warning blast to scare us away."

"Sounds like we should listen to her," the princess said as she looked down toward the castle longingly. "I don't have to actually see this beast to believe you."

"Best idea of the day," said Thand.

The ground began to shake. The vibration jarred several rocks loose. Eschon grabbed Princess Sharman and pushed her aside as a large boulder rolled across their path. A larger, angry, blue flame shot out the cave entrance. This seemed to be more than a simple warning—more like a "leave immediately or I'll roast you" warning.

Oden told them to take cover behind some nearby boulders. When they had done so, he moved up to the cave entrance but stayed to the right, where he was away from any direct blast.

Using the language of the dragon he said, "Nos vilis haud vulnero; we mean no harm." The ground shook again, but this time the dragon's head poked out of the cave entrance and looked on all sides. Oden looked anxious but he stood his ground. The dragon looked at him, then turned its head to the left, where the party was hiding behind the boulders. Eschon couldn't hold back his excitement any longer and leaned out to take a look. The dragon was twenty times the size of a horse. It was covered in red scales and had two white ivory horns sticking out of its head. Without warning, the beast shot a flame directed at Eschon. It glanced off the rock, but the flash singed his hair and left a stinging burn on his hand.

"No, Drächenrød!" Oden screamed. "These are friends."

"It's nothing," Eschon winced. The scorch was more than nothing, but he didn't want this encounter to end. "It's my own fault for not listening."

The dragon, Drächenrød, raised her head high into the air, and sent out a tongue of fire thirty feet long.

Oden turned to the trio and shouted, "Run back to the castle and get Enunciation. Tell him Drächenrød is reacting badly to the strangers. And tell him to bring an ointment for flesh burns."

Thand grabbed Princess Sharman's hand and pulled her back down the trail. He looked back to see his brother still standing behind a rock.

"Go." Oden motioned to Eschon. "It's not safe right now."

Eschon just rolled his shoulders and said, "No. I'm staying."

Drächenrød took several more thunderous steps from the cave, revealing her massive front legs and wings. Most of her body was coated in shiny red scales, but her underbelly looked like a pale yellow hide. Her forelimbs had triple spikes at the shoulders and elbows, and each foot had three clawed toes.

Eschon was overwhelmed with excitement as he stared at the dragon. Pain from the burn barely registered. The dragon turned her head toward him again, and every fragment in his body told him to run. But his brain overruled the terror and replaced it with the need to know.

Smoke drifted from the dragon's nostrils as she sniffed at Oden. Oden made a gesture for Eschon to remain still, then began speaking to Drächenrød in a calm voice. Eschon had no idea what was being said, but the dragon seemed to be listening.

Noises from behind made him turn. Enunciation walked swiftly up the trail with his staff in hand. Thand and Princess Sharman followed, but at a greater distance and much more slowly. As the wizard passed, he motioned Eschon to follow. The hope-to-be wizard took several deep breaths and stepped in behind Enunciation. His shirt was damp and his stomach churned. This was the most exciting thing he had ever done in his life.

Enunciation walked right up to the dragon and slammed his staff on the ground. He began speaking to Drächenrød in a harsh voice. The dragon raised her head into the sky and gave a short blast of fire like she didn't appreciate being commanded, but then lowered her head and began to back into the cave. Once the dragon was fully inside, Enunciation called for Oden and Eschon to follow.

Eschon looked at the dragon's eyes as he walked toward the cave entrance. They were reptilian, with vertical slits. The color was cobalt blue—or maybe more like the color of a lapis lazuli gem.

Clunk. Eschon carelessly tripped over a large animal bone lying on the cave floor. Oden reacted quickly, grabbing his arm and pulling him upright before he hit the ground.

"Be careful," Enunciation reprimanded. "Don't make any sudden movements until Drächenrød is sure that you are not an enemy. Come to me slowly, stand by my side, and try not to show your fear. Dragons have a keen sense for it and will use it to their advantage."

Eschon's legs became weak, and suddenly, he felt the need to sit down. He took a deep breath and forced the fear from his mind. He began to imagine all the possibilities that could come from having the skill to communicate with a dragon. He wanted to learn everything possible about this legendary beast. He wanted to be like Enunciation and reach out to Drächenrød. He stiffened his posture and looked into the dragon's eyes. How lucky could he be to have the privilege of standing in front of a dragon?

An uncontrolled whimper came from behind him. Thand and Princess Sharman stepped warily into the cave, their eyes a mix of fear and amazement.

"I can't believe it," whispered Princess Sharman as she held on tight to Thand's arm.

"Look at that," Thand said in an awed voice. "The real thing."

Drächenrød responded with a low warning growl. Without turning toward them, Enunciation raised his hand. "Stop. Come no farther."

The wizard waited a heartbeat until all was silent and then began to speak once more in the language of dragons.

Sweat rolled down Eschon's face as the primeval creature sniffed him. He thought about his options: surrender to fear, turn and run, or stay and accept the consequences. He tried to remain strong and hold his ground. *I have to pass this test if I'm going to be a wizard. Lip-rot, what am I thinking? I have to pass this test if I'm going to stay alive.*

Then Drächenrød nudged him with her snout, nearly knocking him over. His vision blurred and his heart skipped a beat. For a moment he thought he was going to pass out. But then, the faraway voice of Enunciation cleared his mind as he regained his balance.

"She has accepted you, Eschon; you no longer have to fear her. Now you must touch her near her nose. But stay away from the nostrils; I'm sure they're still hot. Oh, and use the word *amicus* regularly when you talk to her. It means something like *friend*. Oden, you stay here with Eschon and help him adjust to being around Drächenrød. I still have a few loose ends to tie up prior to our leaving tomorrow."

Eschon gingerly touched the dragon's nose. He felt overwhelmed. *She has accepted me.*

Chapter 37

*T*HE CAVE WAS empty now except for Eschon, Oden, and Drächenrød. The drama of their first meeting was over and had been deemed a success. Eschon's resolve had made it possible. The dragon was curled up like a cat, a sign that she no longer felt threatened.

"Well, Eschon, what do you think?" asked Oden.

Eschon looked at the dragon. Her eyeball was more than twice the size of his head. "I don't know what to say. Until now, I've only known dragons through legend. Then, a week ago, a dragon bone was found in Elingale, and now I'm standing next to Drächenrød. It's too exciting to put in words."

"But you must have questions."

"Only a million," Eschon said with a laugh. "Is her flame used only against her enemies?"

Oden pointed to some charred bones scattered about. "No. In fact, dragons use their fire mostly for cooking meals. They're keen on wild game, like deer and gore boar—well-done of course."

Eschon kicked a bone, thinking it might turn to dust. "I would think that after a blast of dragon fire there wouldn't be anything left to eat."

"A dragon has excellent control of its flame. As young dragons, they can only set straw and deadwood on fire. But a mature dragon can roast a pigeon or melt iron with her breath."

Eschon looked at the impressive creature that had now closed her eyes. "What do they do when they're not hunting or eating?"

"Dragons are intelligent creatures that spend much of their time alone in the pursuit of knowledge. They are solitary by nature, preferring to study rather than work. The dragons accumulate their wealth through looting, trade, and barter. They keep their hordes of gems, gold, and silver deep in their caves."

"I don't understand," said Eschon. "Why do they need riches?"

"In reality, they don't. They are powerful enough to take what they want, but they have an inborn trait that compels them to acquire shiny, sparkly things. Dragons are vain, and many use their sticky saliva to apply gemstones to their bodies. Others make ornate breastplates with the dual purpose of protecting their exposed underbellies and displaying their wealth."

Drächenrød made a grumbling noise like she wanted them to go.

"I think it's time we leave her," said Oden. "We don't want to push our luck. Keep in mind that they like to be alone."

As soon as Eschon reached the castle, he dashed down corridors, sticking his head through doorways, until he finally found Enunciation working in a small room, packing a leather bag with bottles of powder and oil.

"I have a thousand questions," he said breathlessly to the wizard.

"Oh, I almost forgot. Let me look at that burn on your hand."

Eschon had forgotten about the burn but stuck his hand out as he asked, "How do dragons make fire?"

Enunciation looked closely at the wound and then gently

dabbed oil on the scorched skin. "That's a good question. It shows me you're thinking. Dragons have two very large lungs. One holds oxygen like humans, and the other contains the gas methane. When the two are combined, you have fire.

Eschon lowered his hand. "How do—"

"Hold your questions for now. We are leaving tonight for Aerie Castle, and if you want to be my apprentice, you need to be ready to fly. I assume Thand knows your plans."

Eschon spun and looked out the window. "Fly! We're going to fly on the dragon?"

"Of course, how do you think I got here?"

"Well, I hadn't thought about it. But Thand has been to your castle, and he didn't fly on a dragon. He rode a horse."

Enunciation pinched his eyebrows, as if it were too many questions. "That takes too long. Now, I'm not going to discuss this with you. If you're going to be a grand wizard, you will have to learn to deal with dragons. If you wish to come by horse, then I'll assume that you just want to be a common magician."

Eschon spun back from the window. "No, no, I want to be a great wizard. Just like you."

"Good, then go get your things and meet me here one hour after sunset."

"Why after sundown? Why not know?"

The wizard stopped and crossed his arms. "It seems that I am going to be hounded by questions. It's best if a dragon stays out of view during daylight hours. Can you imagine how the people would react if they saw a dragon flying around? Most would flee in panic, but a few would get their weapons and shoot at her."

"Then why not leave at sundown? Why do we have to wait an hour?"

"She usually takes the first hour after dark to feed herself.

Believe me; you don't want to fly on a hungry dragon. They dart all over the place, looking for food, and they ignore your commands. Then, after the hunt, you'll have to sit and watch while she eats. You'll never get home."

The wizard walked over to Eschon and put a hand on his shoulder. "It's time you get ready. You'll want to say goodbye to everyone. It may be a while before you see them again."

Eschon found Thand brooding in his room. He cleared his throat and then walked in hesitantly. "Thand, I'm going to leave tonight, with Enunciation. We're going to fly back to Mount Aerie. I don't know how long I'll be gone, but I won't be returning anytime soon."

Thand looked back with a vacant stare. The dark circles under his eyes had become noticeable.

Eschon showed Thand a folded piece of paper. "This is for Mother. It explains what I'm doing and why."

He stepped closer. "I'm sorry that I hurt your feelings. I want to make things right before I leave. Sometimes I wish we could go back to the old days, when it was just you and me and Mother harassing Lord Creedy. Life was simple then."

Like a bomb exploding, Thand jumped up. "Go! Leave. But don't think things will be the same when you return. Soon I'll have the feather again, and my power will be great. You had your chance. Remember that."

Chapter 38

ESCHON WALKED ALONE in the dark, wondering if he was sleepwalking or moving toward the most significant day of his life. Even in his fantasies, where mythical creatures and legends were true, dragon riding seemed impossible. A tingling mixture of exhilaration and anxiety had him in front of the hillside cave twenty minutes early.

His mentor was standing in front of the cave.

"I'm ready to ride," he fibbed. "Just say the word."

Enunciation looked at the boy and smiled. "I see you're a little early, but that's okay. Just stand to the side while I call Drächenrød. Be silent and don't make any sudden movements. Where is Thand?"

"I don't know, but the princess said she'd watch from down the hill. No closer."

"Still cautious. That's not a bad thing when it comes to dragons."

Enunciation turned and started speaking the language of the dragon. The ground began to tremble, and unhurriedly Drächenrød emerged from the cave. She sniffed the air, then turned toward Eschon, then turned back to the wizard. For the first time, Eschon saw the dragon in her full glory. Her garnet-red scales were thick and shiny and sparkled brightly, even in the torchlight. The leather-like wings were red on top but pale yellow on the bottom. A swishing sound caused Eschon to jump high as the dragon's long, tapered tail swept under him.

Oden emerged from the cave, dusting his hands. "Good reflexes."

He turned toward Enunciation. "She's saddled and ready to ride. I made some adjustments to accommodate Eschon."

Eschon studied Drächenrød. Between the saddle and the dragon's back lay a rich purple cloth embroidered with yellow symbols of enchantment. The dual seat was made from new leather dyed to the color of blood. Two sets of stirrups, made of silver, were attached to the seat by gold-braided straps. On the top of the saddle, a pair of ivory carved saddle horns gave the riders something to grip. Firelight glimmered off the sapphires, emeralds, and diamonds that outlined the saddle flap.

Eschon bent over and examined the underbelly of the dragon. There was a scaled breastplate made of solid gold with the face of Drächenrød etched in silver. Two large rubies represented her eyes. The dragon was frighteningly beautiful, and by the way she moved and held her head high, she knew it.

He stood again. "She looks spectacular. The breastplate is amazing."

"The dragon's underbelly is tough, but not like the scaled areas on top. The armor plate is made of gold to reflect light back into her enemy's eyes, and the jewels are there to show the world that she has so much wealth that she can place jewels on her armor.

"Now, place your things in that saddlebag. Oden will pass it up to us once we're seated."

Oden pulled over a nine-step wooden platform constructed specifically for mounting the dragon. Enunciation climbed the steps first, put his foot in the stirrup, and swung his leg to the other side. He made some adjustments and when he looked relatively comfortable, he called for Eschon.

Eschon had grown accustomed to humans being taller, but against the dragon, he felt minuscule. And as if to magnify that difference, he had to ask Oden for a boost. His legs were spread wide across the saddle, and his inside thigh muscles burned already from the unnatural stretch.

Oden performed a few more adjustments to seat him properly. "No one said that this ride would be comfortable. Just try to enjoy the experience and forget the rest."

Eschon's heart was in his throat from the tension and exhilaration. He could feel the warm flesh moving below him. Oden moved the platform away from the dragon and asked Eschon one more time if he was okay. The young apprentice gave a nervous nod, and then Enunciation leaned forward and whispered something to Drächenrød.

The dragon took a step forward, and they shifted to the side. The movement scared Eschon. But before he could say anything, the dragon took another step, and they shifted the other way. Eschon began to doubt if he would be able to stay in the saddle.

Then Drächenrød began loping toward the cliff's edge, throwing Eschon back and forth, up and down. Fear replaced excitement; he couldn't stop her, and he didn't think he could hold on.

Suddenly, Drächenrød vaulted into the sky. Eschon was slung backward for a second and then downward, as the dragon's weight pulled them back toward the earth. In the next instant the dragon extended her wings, and for a moment they were floating on a sea of air. The euphoric feeling ended when the red dragon pushed its wings downward. A jerky, up-and-down motion followed as they slowly gained altitude. Eschon's dread of dropping off was replaced by his previously unknown fear of heights.

It was a rough few minutes, but he finally synced with all of the motion and looked down. Torches lit the perimeter of Princess

Sharman's castle. For the first time, he saw it as a whole unit—no longer just rooms and walls. Ahead, the mountain ridge was rimmed in the fading orange light. Above, the white stars lay on a blanket of black silk. Suddenly, he remembered his brother and glanced below, but only saw darkness.

Eschon could tell they were gaining height by the tilt of Drächenrød's head. As the dragon soared above the landscape, the flapping motion became smoother.

The wind streamed through his hair, and the temperature started to chill. To keep warm, he reached for the shawl that was given to him by Princess Sharman. She'd said it was made for dragon riders, but the grin on her face had told him it was probably hers.

The air continued to grow colder, and breathing became more difficult. After a while he grew so cold that he had to mention it to Enunciation. The wizard told him that there was a wool cloak in the saddlebag. Carefully, he unbuckled the bag and removed the garment. But just as he was placing it on, Drächenrød shot downward and turned sharply. Eschon's stomach leaped into his mouth, and he reached for the wizard's back. The cloak and shawl went flying into the darkness. It wasn't until they regained level flight that he realized they were gone.

Tears formed and his teeth began chattering. He drew a deep breath and tapped Enunciation on the shoulder. "I've lost the cape. I thought we were falling and I foolishly let go of the cape trying to steady myself."

Enunciation looked over his shoulder and said, "Well, there's nothing that can be done about it now."

"I'm sorry. I should have trusted you and Drächenrød."

"You'll just have to endure. If you keep low, behind my back, it won't be as windy."

Eschon hunched low, but the difference was minimal. He squeezed his body tight, yet his teeth still chattered. It wasn't long before his whole body began to shake violently. Silently, he suffered the bitter cold.

A short time later Enunciation turned his head and said, "I have an idea." Then he spoke into the dragon's ear. All of a sudden, the sky brightened and a blast of warmth passed over the two. Eschon felt the difference immediately. After a few more blasts of warm air, his shaking went back to just teeth rattling.

"She can't do this continuously, but every once in a while, she'll give you a roar."

About two hours into the flight, Eschon began to feel the pressure in his ears change and saw that the tilt of the dragon's head had shifted lower. Enunciation informed him it wouldn't be long now. Shortly thereafter, Drächenrød stopped her periodic flapping and tilted sharply to the right. They began to spiral down.

Because of the darkness, Eschon had no idea what was happening, but their forward momentum began to slow drastically. Then Drächenrød leveled out, shifted her wings, and immediately began back-flapping. Within seconds there was a hard *thump*, and the seat began to shift right and left again as the dragon walked into a cave.

Several torches were already lit inside, and there was a man waiting to help them dismount. Eschon climbed down and went toward the torch to warm his hands. He walked with a waddle, but he felt taller and stronger, like he had conquered the world. Sharing this experience with Thand would have been nice, but that would have to wait for another time.

The wizard and his new apprentice walked out the front of the cave as Drächenrød went deeper into the side of the mountain.

Then, without any warning, a bright light and fireball blasted from the cave.

"Never linger in a dragon cave, Eschon."

Chapter 39

*T*HAND TOSSED THE blanket back and moved to the edge of the bed. A rumble in his stomach was a reminder that he hadn't been eating. For several nights, sleep had been elusive. Eschon had flown off to Aerie Mountain, and he didn't know when they would meet again. *I shouldn't have talked to him that way. If there was some way to take it back, I would.*

He walked around the room several times, rubbing the back of his neck. Then, sitting in a chair next to the desk, he scrubbed a hand over his face. *Why can't I relax? I'm always thinking about that bedamn feather. I need to get home, back to the feather. Give me some more time and I'll figure out how to use it. Then I'll show them how wrong they are.*

The afternoon was scheduled for training. Thand walked to the practice ring, willing himself to be positive. He had to accept Cayman or quit. He was no quitter, so he'd try to tolerate Cayman's instructions.

Despite believing he had put his ill feeling behind him, Thand's chest was tight when he arrived at the arena. Cayman was down on one knee adjusting some equipment and didn't bother to look up when he walked over to him.

I guess I deserve this. Why should I expect a greeting from a fighting instructor?

"Cayman, I regret my rudeness from the other day," Thand said in a voice that was barely louder than a whisper. He meant to be louder but his throat constricted. Cayman could have easily ignored the halfhearted apology, but he stood up and nodded in acceptance.

Princess Sharman walked over. "It must be a good day. You two are talking."

Thand took her hand in his but looked down. "I'm sorry I didn't talk to you earlier about . . ." He glanced over at Cayman, then back. "You know what I'm talking about."

"Yes. I'm sorry you don't trust me. Isn't that what you meant to say?"

Thand sighed. "Yes. I should've told you sooner."

Princess Sharman nodded and let go of his hand, then picked up her practice sword. Thand did the same, but before he took his ready position, Princess Sharman took a swing at the back of his legs, hitting him behind the knees. Thand's legs buckled, and he collapsed into the dirt.

Stunned by her action, he looked up at her with a questioning expression. She reached down, pulled him upward, leaned in, and whispered, "Now we're even." Then she pecked him on the cheek.

Touching the spot of her kiss, he wondered what was going on.

Cayman seemed amused by the spectacle and asked where his kiss was. She walked over and pecked him on the cheek. "Now you're even with Thand."

Thand's hands dropped to his side. *Was that meant to provoke me?* Determined to stick to his resolve, he decided to ignore the flirtation.

For the next hour they practiced with their wooden swords.

Cut to the neck, parry high right; cut to the knee, parry low right. Thand was tense and his timing was poor. Repel, evade, attack—his blocks and parries were sluggish. Several times he had to be reminded to focus. Pressure was building behind his eyes. A headache was forming. Finally, he asked Cayman to call a time-out; the heat and his performance were combining to infuriate him.

Princess Sharman walked to the water bucket, dipped the ladle into tub, and drank the cool water. Then she drew another and handed it to Cayman.

Thand just stared. *What about me? Is she trying to start something?*

Princess Sharman must have seen his reaction. She put a hand on her hip. "You can have one too," she said, handing him the empty ladle.

She dipped it for him. Why not me?

"No thanks," he said sarcastically.

There was only one shady spot in the arena, so the three of them were forced to sit together. He couldn't think of anything positive to say, so he remained silent. Sharman and Cayman seemed unperturbed by his silence and chatted about her injury. At one point, she turned her back to him and opened the top button of her blouse, exposing her shoulder so that Cayman could see her scar. He commented on how well it was healing. Then she rebuttoned her shirt and began asking Cayman about the investigation.

Thand's head was pounding, his vision blurry. Finally, he stood and shouted, "Are we here to learn how to defend ourselves, or have I missed the purpose of this get-together?"

Cayman stood up. "Break's over. We're going to work on

protecting ourselves when we don't have a weapon. Thand, I want you to take all that pent-up anger and swing at me."

Thand stood back, his bottom lip trembling, and then released his repressed rage by thrusting his fist headlong into Cayman's jaw.

Cayman put up his left hand and shoved Thand's right arm to the side, using a blocking move. The punch slid by Cayman's head without doing any damage. Thand stumbled but kept upright.

Princess Sharman was asked to do the same. But as her arm came forward, Cayman grabbed it and pushed it up over her head, grabbed her waist, and pulled her tight to his own body. He smiled and then released her.

Thand gave him a steely look and said, "Unless that's a dance move, it really isn't effective. If you had done that to me, I would have driven my knee into your groin."

"That would be a good countermove, Thand. Now, come at me again."

Thand's anger overpowered his resolve, and he charged. At the last second, Cayman stepped to the side and swept his leg under Thand's, thumping him to the ground.

Stunned, Thand lay on his back wheezing, laboring to get air in his lungs. The princess rushed to his side, put her hand behind his head, and lifted him into a sitting position.

Blood trickled down Thand's neck as he pushed her aside. He tried to stand and face Cayman, but his spinning head wouldn't allow him to stand.

The princess held him still. "Please, stop this. This has gone too far. Cayman, get me some water."

Cayman hurried and brought the whole bucket back. "I'm

sorry, Thand. That was stupid of me. I was showing off instead of teaching."

She gave Thand a drink from the ladle and then dipped her scarf in the water to clean his wound. "Are you all right? I'm sorry, too. I didn't think my childish behavior would hurt anyone. Please forgive me."

Princess Sharman tied the scarf around his head. His cheeks were on fire as he trembled with humiliation. Suddenly, his composure disintegrated. Jumping up, he threw the bandage at her feet and staggered away.

Thand did not go back to training for several days. He used his injury as an excuse, but the truth was he couldn't face anyone. His spirits were low, and there was no doubt that everyone in the castle was looking at him differently. He was sure they were following him, hoping he would lead them to his feather. Once, he had felt like this castle was a second home, but now he couldn't feel more like an outsider than if he was a beggar.

Princess Sharman had a tray of food sent to his room each day. Each night the tray was picked up, the food untouched.

Sitting in his room, nursing the head wound, he had a chance to put all of the pieces together.

"Now I get it," he said, looking out the window. "She's doing this deliberately, trying to drive me away. I'm not good enough for her. I'm too short, have pointed ears, and have no formal education. Well, if the princess thinks like that, after all we have been through together, she's just a narrow-minded commoner. From now on it's 'Sharman,' not 'Princess.' She's not worthy of the title. Twila, too."

Chapter 40

ESPITE THE PHYSICAL and emotional drain of dragon flying, Eschon was up at dawn, anxious to see his new home in daylight. The smell of fresh bread baking in a stone oven guided him to the kitchen.

The cook laid out a simple meal of fruit and sweet bread, telling him that Enunciation had already eaten and would be back shortly. He looked around the kitchen and his shoulders drooped as he thought about his mother. She enjoyed cooking and would love to have a kitchen like this. He gawked at the fireplace. It was big enough to roast two pigs at once. The stone oven was so large that a half a dozen loaves could be baked at the same time. There was even a well in the corner. No running outside in bad weather to fetch water.

Eschon scrubbed a hand over his face. Now that the thrill of dragon riding had subsided, he realized how isolated he was. All his friends were in Elingale. His brother, the princess, Cayman, and Oden were all at Adrianna Castle. He gave a heavy sigh. *I hope I made the right decision.*

Eschon flinched at a noise from behind his back. With an unsmiling face, he turned and looked at the wizard.

The wizard gave him an understanding smile and then said, "I told you it would be a lonely job."

Eschon sat up straight, hoping to dispel his forlorn look. "I'm okay."

Enunciation put a hand on his shoulder. "Your face tells me another story, but I'll keep you so busy that you won't have time to think about anything else. Now, are you ready to explore? After all, this will be your new home for some time."

Eschon shook the sadness away with a vigorous nod. Within minutes, he was badgering the wizard with questions. "How old is the castle? How long have you lived here?"

"More questions," Enunciation said. "Slow down. Listen and observe. All answers will be revealed in time."

The tour revealed lofty ceilings and wide hallways. The dimensions of the rooms and the leaded glass windows told a story of grandeur. But the cobweb corners, ashless fireplaces, and a taint of decay told another tale.

Eschon didn't want to say it out loud, but he was disappointed in what he saw. He had something like King Treutlen's castle in mind when he arrived in the dark the night before. After all, Enunciation was a great man, and he expected a great castle.

Enunciation stopped the tour for a moment. "Do I see disappointment on your face?"

Eschon flushed. "No. Well, maybe a little. But it sure beats anything I've ever lived in."

Enunciation gave a crisp nod. "Most of this castle is a huge waste of space, filled with useless rooms. It's not what I wanted. The east tower with its laboratory, library, and observatory was what I really needed. But the offer was the entire castle or nothing. King Treutlen made it difficult for me to refuse."

Enunciation began walking again. "He promised me unlimited

support with my experiments. All the daily needs would be taken care of by the staff."

Eschon was relieved that the wizard hadn't taken offense. "That sounds like a pretty generous offer."

"Yes, it was. But if you intend to be a great wizard, you must understand that there is always a motive behind a generous offer. I think the king really wanted a secure holding on this side of the mountain, maintained by a strong ally. You know, in the event that he had to deal with another rebellion."

"A rebellion? Against what?" questioned Eschon.

"Enough," said Enunciation. "That's a story for another time. Let's go to my favorite part of the castle."

The wizard suddenly became energized, so much so that he got ahead of Eschon. The new apprentice ran down the hall, turned a corner, and there was Enunciation, standing in a corridor, bathed in bright light. For a moment he looked like he was from the spirit world. After roaming through dark passageways, the contrast in light made Eschon squint. He blinked several times, then walked to the normal-looking wizard.

"This is your bridge to a new life," said Enunciation, and he pointed toward a fully enclosed overpass. Sunshine beamed in through long, crystal-clear windows and illuminated a beautiful, ribbed vault ceiling. Light bounced off a polished oak floor, which connected the old castle to a modernistic tower.

The bridge spanned a thousand-foot chasm. He hesitated, as if stepping onto the crossway might change his life forever. Enunciation smiled a knowing look, then took him by the elbow and led him to a window. The view was spectacular. Smoky-blue mountaintops reached into the sky. Hundred-foot pine trees appeared as blades of grass. In the near distance, a rainbow arched above a waterfall that cascaded thousands of feet down the mountainside before disappearing behind the landscape.

"Follow me," the wizard said, as an elaborately carved door opened silently. Eschon's eyebrows rose.

"Just some basic magic. That door's become too heavy."

They stepped past the rune-covered entry and into an enormous room. The walls were lined with books, maps, and a sphere that rested on a pedestal. Unlike other parts of the castle, this area was bright, clean, and well maintained.

Enunciation led Eschon toward the far end, where the room angled to the right. The wizard swept his arm toward the opening and motioned for his new apprentice to go first.

Eschon's eyes swept the room like an owl. A concave wall was lined from floor to ceiling with glass panels. Green marble columns supported a vaulted ceiling, painted to simulate the dawning day. On the east side of the dome, a curved panel of glass rose to the center of the ceiling. The morning sun ascended along the opening until it reached the top of the dome at high noon. The dome also moved to account for the seasonal changes of the sun path.

The wizard seemed to glow with pride. "This is my favorite room. It's designed to inspire new ideas. Walk over to the window and look at the view."

Eschon walked to the window's edge and looked out to where the peaks touched the sky. His eyes followed the slope of the mountain downward. Unexpectedly, he became dizzy.

"Whoa!" Eschon closed his eyes and backed away. "I feel like I'm falling."

The room protruded from the castle's wall in such a manner that only emptiness was visible below his feet.

"It's called vertigo, but that's not the effect I had intended when I built it. Yet everyone but me seems to suffer the same feeling." Enunciation pointed to a comfortable, high-back leather chair. "Please take a seat. I promise the room is not going to fall into the valley."

Eschon took a seat that faced the window. The wizard sat in a chair next to him and said, "I think of this space as a room where your imagination can soar beyond its earthbound thoughts, as a launching point or a catapult for new ideas. I can sit here all day contemplating the possibilities."

Eschon moved to the edge of his chair. If he was beginning a new life, he felt compelled to come clean with Enunciation. Leaning forward in a conspiratorial gesture, he said, "Since you're in a thoughtful mood, I'd like to speak with you about my brother. It begins with him finding the Kookachoo Bird's feather."

Enunciation's eyes widened. "Is that so? You really think it's the feather? Have you seen it?"

"Yes, and it fits the description perfectly. But so far the feather hasn't done much except change Thand's personality."

Eschon shifted in his seat. "He used to be up at first light, fishing or hunting. Then he'd arrive at the fields for a day of work. Now he stays in his room, alone, coming out only when required. His confidence and determination have been replaced by doubt and insecurity. He has become jealous of every man who goes near the princess—especially Cayman."

Eschon stood, walked to the fireplace, and then turned to face the wizard. The warmth on his back was comforting.

"When he first found the feather, he talked about the wonderful things that he could accomplish. He even thought it might be useful against Baylock, if he ever showed up again. Now all he thinks about is how to use it for his own purpose. The power of the feather is eating him away like rust on a sword. Isn't there some kind of spell or potion we could concoct to return him to his old self?"

The wizard gave an understanding nod. "If only it was that easy. Magic can change elemental objects, but not personalities. We could use a spell to trick him into believing something has changed, but it would be better for everyone if Thand realized how much he's transformed since finding the feather. I know Thand. He is not normally self-centered. So it is likely that he can return to himself—but not without guidance. You must become the big brother and steer him back to his natural personality."

Eschon gave a hesitant nod and then sat down again. "I'm not sure. It will be hard to change his mind. It just happened too fast. The feather must have some magical quality that has taken control of him."

"The perceived power of the feather can twist one's thinking." Enunciation put his hand on Eschon's knee. "The ability to control other people's lives, to have them do your bidding, is very corrosive. Most men fail at this, and soon their needs become greater than the people's. This is common when someone suddenly acquires power. If Thand could see how greed has changed him, he would be ashamed of himself. He has a good heart, so it is likely he can regain himself before he goes too far. It's your duty as a brother to help him back."

"Maybe he can come to you. He thinks that all he needs to do is learn a few words of magic and then the feather will do his bidding. If that's true, maybe you can help him," said Eschon.

"It's possible, but I'd have to do a lot of research on the feather to learn its purpose. I'm sure it wasn't designed to just spew out whatever the holder wishes. It probably has the capacity to guide the holder toward good decisions that will lead to wealth and prosperity. Expecting it to be a slave to your every wish is misguided."

"Try convincing Thand of that."

Chapter 41

I'M ALMOST THERE, Baylock thought as he gathered his notes in the library. *Soon, the world will comprehend my power and cower.* His endeavor to command the spoken word was paying off. He looked to a sunny spot on the floor. His trusty dog, Caedo, was curled in a circle, soaking up the warmth of the afternoon sun. "Determination, Caedo. Remember, you can't achieve success without it."

He slid the papers into a folder labeled Afaisha Spell. This was the name for his newest conjuration. It was derived from the word *agraphia*, a disease of the central nervous system that affects the ability to communicate.

Caedo stood up, sensing that his master was going to leave. Baylock walked out of the room, feeling a sense of calm and ease that hadn't been there for weeks. He called for his new assistant, Sedgley.

Sedgley had initially been unhappy living on Skull Island. He didn't like being constrained to the interior of the Cranium, but when Baylock told him about the creatures outside, there was no other choice. Since then, he had learned to navigate the island during daylight hours without any incidents. But even if he could get to the shoreline, no ship was capable of coming close to the island.

"Sedgley, we need to put together a small army of about fifty men, and we'll need a captain with his own ship. How many people from Whistler Key do you think you can recruit?"

Finding sailors that would work for Baylock wouldn't be hard if he paid them right. But finding a captain could be more difficult. Very few of them owned their own ship. Since most of skippers were just employees of a shipping company, the use of a ship for personal gain would be an act of piracy.

"Well, that depends on how much you're willing to pay. I can get quite a few men for the right price."

"Will four copper coins buy a good army?"

Sedgley scoffed. "No, you cheapskate. But two gold coins will get you as many men as you need, and three gold coins will get you the type that can lead these mercenaries. And just so you can budget right, my fee is three gold coins plus two silver."

The color in Baylock's face grew red. "For someone with no options, you're a contrary little rascal."

"You'll find no one better suited for this job than me. And remember, a dead man can't help you."

Baylock liked this brassy man. He was arrogant but usually right. And it was refreshing to have someone around him who wasn't afraid to speak up. He'd let the comment slide.

"Sedgley, money won't be a problem once I've completed my spell."

"Good. Now that you've made an honest confession, my fee will be four gold coins."

"You're annoying me. Have I ever taken you out to see my pet spider Mactabilis? He works for nothing but food."

"Just kidding, Your Wizardship. I'll be happy to take whatever your generous heart decides."

"Watch the words you speak to me, Sedgley. The wrong one can end your life."

The crossing was uneventful that day. Calm seas and a steady west wind made sailing practically effortless. The plan was for Sedgley to scour the docks for a captain and crew, then send them to Baylock, who would spend the day in comfort at Gerard's Tavern. Why waste a day baking in the hot sun when Sedgley could do the work? A well-trained army wasn't needed, just a bunch of thugs who could intimidate. At the wage he was paying, Sedgley should have no trouble finding them.

Baylock handed him a few coins to tempt the recruits and warned him that he must keep the name of the island secret.

"Like I don't already know," he replied.

Behind the waterfront were storefronts of all sorts. A doctor's office, a spice merchant, and a jeweler were located along Tavern Road. Palm trees shaded the lane of hard-packed sand, making walking a simple task.

Baylock turned into the sprawling inn and tavern and was greeted by Gerard. He required a separate room with food and plenty of ale.

"To set aside a room would be costly," the tavern owner told him. "It means I'd have to turn customers away."

Baylock set a bag of coins on the table and opened it. "How much?"

The day had progressed nicely. Men had started arriving within an hour, and by late afternoon he had his crew. He sealed the deal with each man by buying each a cup of ale and paying him three days worth of wages to travel back to his island. Now all he needed was a captain.

Late in the afternoon, Sedgley walked in the room with a potential captain. Baylock did not like what he saw. The man's hair was pulled back and tied in a knot so tight that his skin was without a wrinkle. The captain was as tall as a ship's mast and skinny as a rope. He shuffled over to the wizard on spindly legs, with his nose arriving long before the rest of his face. In a shrill voice, he introduced himself as Captain Tiger.

Baylock tried not to laugh. "What are your qualifications?"

"I was educated and trained by the Royal Navy of Switzany."

"Never heard of it."

Sedgley jumped in. "Well qualified, Your Wizardship. I have questioned him thoroughly. He's won many naval battles, but his greatest qualification is that he possesses his own ship. Not many out there that does."

Baylock was a little skeptical. If his ship looked anything like him, they were in trouble. "Let me see the vessel."

Baylock walked to the appropriate pier while the new crew straggled behind. The vessel was a medium-sized, twin-masted ship. There were two decks below the main, and it could store eighty barrels in the hold while still carrying the men. Baylock walked around the ship, looking for rot. Climbing on board, he examined the ropes, inspected the sails, and finally declared it seaworthy.

When the large number of men began boarding the new ship, several nearby ship captains came running toward him. A confrontation seemed inevitable.

"Who are you, and what are you doing here?" the biggest man yelled.

"How are we to maintain our ships without a crew?" said another.

Baylock told them it wasn't his problem and that they should pay their men more money.

"We don't set the wages. The company does."

An argument with the wizard ensued, and it soon grew heated. One captain pulled his flintlock pistol and another pulled his sword. Suddenly, the moisture in the air evaporated, and a powerful jet of water shot from Baylock's right hand, striking the pistol and knocking it into the water. The sword-swinging captain raced toward him screaming, but Baylock shifted his aim and disarmed the man just as efficiently.

A second group of men rushed toward Baylock. With his left hand, he discharged a wide arc of energy that flattened them. The show of power was enough for everyone to stop and retreat to their ships. His men finished boarding, while congratulating themselves as if they had something to do with the outcome. The other ships were not a problem after seeing that. There were only a few shouts and curses from the sailors left behind.

Baylock was concerned that the hostile captains would seek retaliation. Maybe they would follow him out to sea and attack with their cannons. As his crew raised the sails, he put a ward around the bay, locking all ships into the harbor until the next sunrise.

They navigated out of the harbor and headed for the open sea. Sedgley saw two ships hoist their sails as if they planned to give chase. He alerted the wizard, who just laughed and said, "Too bad we won't see the look on their faces when they hit the invisible barrier."

The men were in a good mood. Their pockets were full of coin. Some were in awe of his display of power. Others whispered that they had met stronger magicians than him.

The sun was beginning its dip into the western horizon when Skull Island became visible. A ripple of fear went through the men and rumors started flying. When the ship cleared the point, it became obvious that Skull Island was the destination.

One of the sailors walked up to Sedgley. "How stupid is this guy? He's sailing us right into Skull Island."

Sedgley told the man to shut up, but it was too late. Baylock had heard the words.

Angered by the insolence, he walked right up to the man, and without a word, he chopped him in the throat with the edge of his hand. The man fell to the deck gagging. His throat began to swell, blocking his air passage. His face turned blue as he struggled for air.

"Look over the side," the magician commanded the crew. "This is what happens to anyone who dares to speak against me."

Effortlessly, he lifted the man from the deck and tossed him into the sea. The thrashing and screaming ended quickly in a pool of red.

"A warning to all of you: words have consequences."

Chapter 42

*T*HE WEIGHT OF responsibility was pulling Cayman down. The tightness in his chest was becoming chronic; puffiness had appeared below his eyes.

The assassin was still roaming free, and Cayman seemed to be failing as an instructor. Thand was no longer attending practice, and the princess only showed up sporadically. His confidence was shredded like a torn sail. But quitting wasn't an option. He had faced adversity before.

Today he was going to question Lord Creedy, a doubtful suspect in his mind. It wasn't that he lacked motive; it was that he lacked opportunity. Locked away in the ship's jail was a pretty strong alibi. But it was possible that Creedy had made arrangements before he was imprisoned. A former Creedy employee had disclosed his boss' promise to destroy Princess Sharman for her involvement with the Elwins.

The prison was located in a cold, damp, subterranean vault two levels below the main floor of the castle. Cayman stopped at the guardroom and informed the watchman that he would be meeting with the prisoner. The hatchet-faced guard grabbed a torch and led the way down a steep, winding staircase. The walls were damp and frigid, the air moldy with the smell of decay. The notion of being buried alive came to mind.

They walked past several iron doors with prisoners too sick or comatose to care. The guard put the torch in a wrought-iron bracket and unlocked the door.

The warden crinkled his nose. "I'll wait for you at the top of the stairs. It's too evil-smelling down here for my delicate sense of smell. Ha!"

Cayman pushed open the door and set eyes on a pasty-skinned, skeletal man. It seemed that he had aged twenty years since first seeing him locked in the brig on Trident Sea. A ceiling light illuminated the cell with a bluish-green glow, adding to his pallor. The mysterious light, about the size of two bricks, was mounted flush in the ceiling. It must have been an enchanted lamp since it produced no heat. The perpetual light was intentional, he'd learned. If the passage of time was impossible to track, then the prisoner would be weakened and disoriented—less likely to try an escape.

Creedy sat on a pallet, wearing a coarse brown robe tied off with a double length of hemp rope. The jailers called it the suicide robe because there was enough rope to hang oneself. His bare feet were dirt black.

"Nice to see you again," Creedy wheezed. The words triggered a coughing fit that came from deep within his chest.

"Yes, thank yuh." Cayman had previously decided that playing to his vanity might produce better results. "I'm here to seek advice, not to question your innocence. There's no way yuh could have done it, but who do yuh think would want to kill the princess?"

"Yes, that's the big question," Creedy said in between fits of coughing. "Get me out of here. I'll give you names and money." After another coughing spasm, he spit out a glob of blood. "Despite your sugary statement, I know you doubt my innocence.

But you're wrong. I was in the brig when it happened. It was impossible for me to shoot that arrow."

"I agree, but that doesn't mean yuh not involved in some way or don't know who's responsible."

Creedy turned to his right and mumbled as if he were talking to the wall. He turned back to Cayman. "I must consult my friend behind the wall. You see, these walls are alive. They listen, they talk, and they have stories to tell and secrets to keep."

"You're going mad, Creedy. Confinement will do that. If you answer my questions, I can get them to move yuh to a better jail above ground, with a window and fresh air. Now, tell me. What information do yuh have?"

Iron clinked against stone as Creedy stood, but the metal leg shackles limited his range so that he was not a threat. "I know who's responsible for the attack on the princess."

"Of course yuh do. That's why I'm here. Give me a name and I'll send a doctor."

Creedy laughed. "You're a fool. The most likely suspect is rarely the murderer. He set it up to make me look like the assassin. But he didn't expect me to have a perfect alibi. Help me escape and I'll give you the killer."

Cayman pretended to pick a piece of lint off of his sleeve. "Yuh know it doesn't matter to me if I find the killer. It's no skin off my nose, one way or the other. I didn't even know the princess until a few weeks ago, so why should I care? Sure, it'll make me look good if I find him. But other than a pat on the back, there's nothing in it for me."

"You're a bad liar. I know you have a soft spot for her. Let me out of here, and I'll give you the killer and make you rich. And you'll have the princess in your debt forever."

"And the blame for your escape. No, I don't trust yuh. What

will stop yuh from just running off? Tell me what happened and then I'll help."

Lord Creedy shook his head. "And what will stop you from leaving me here if I give you the information?"

Cayman shrugged his shoulders. "Have it your way then." He turned and walked to the iron door. "It looks like our mutual distrust has made this meeting useless. Let me know if yuh change your mind."

The guard was called, and Creedy sat down with a heavy sigh. In a sad voice that was almost imperceptible, he whispered to the wall, "You should have told him about the hidden note."

Cayman spun, walked back, and kneeled in front of Creedy, ignoring the filth. "What note? What are you talking about?"

Creedy coughed right in Cayman's face. Cayman stood and wiped his arm across his face. "I'll assume that was an accident. Now, tell me about this note. I'll have the doctor come right now."

"Get me a doctor and I'll give you a clue. Help me escape and I'll give you the assassin."

Cayman sighed. *How many more times is he going to ask me to get him out of here?*

"If I think your information is good enough, I'll call for the healer. And I'll tell the king you helped. Now, tell me what you know."

Cayman had just left a meeting with Oden and the king when Princess Sharman came running up to him. "Have you had any luck tracking the assassin?"

"I visited Lord Creedy in the dungeon. His health is poor and his mind is shot. He still won't admit to anything, but he said he knows who did it. If the king gives him a pardon, he'll talk. But it's not going to happen."

She placed her hand on her chest and said, "Good. I'm not sure I want Lord Creedy roaming free."

"I spoke to your father a few minutes ago, and just the mention of setting Creedy free made him angry: 'After what that criminal did to my daughter. You think I'm going to let him go free? No, absolutely not. There's still one assassin roaming this island. If I free him there would be two.' Creedy did give me an unclear message about a note hidden in his house, but he wouldn't say any more without his freedom being guaranteed."

"So, what's going to happen next?"

"We're preparing the ship for a return to Lapis Lazuli. We leave the day after tomorrow. You and Thand are expected to be on it."

Chapter 43

THAND CLAPPED HIS hands together when he heard the news. Returning to Lapis Lazuli was just what he wanted. Leaving home had turned into a disaster. For some reason he didn't understand, everyone had turned against him. But in three days he'd be home and reunited with his feather. The skin on his arm tingled when he thought about holding it once again. *I'll discover the magic of the feather this time, and I'll show them all!*

Then a wave of fear washed over him. *Discover the feather? What if somebody came into the house? What if Baylock came back and found it? Baylock! His magic plus the power of the feather would make him unstoppable.*

On the day they set sail, the clouds were heavy with rain. Looking to the distance, the ocean and sky merged into a pallet of black and gray.

The *Trident Seas'* ropes were untied from the mooring posts, and she began moving down the river. By the time they entered the open sea, torrents of rain were sweeping the deck. Unlike a thunderstorm that comes in noisy and leaves quickly, this storm had been building for days and was now beginning to unleash its fury.

A curtain of rain fell from the sky and reduced visibility so that the land became invisible. Angry gray clouds and stormy gray water seemed to swallow them whole.

The waves grew larger as they moved farther into the open water. The ship rose thirty feet on a wave and then plunged down, only to be lifted up by another wave. All the while, it rocked from side to side. Sailors spoke of Neptune's wrath and displayed their evil eye charms to drive away the hellish storm.

The risk of washing overboard was very real, and the captain wanted no repeats of the incident near Skull Island. Only essential personnel were allowed on deck, which left Thand and Princess Sharman trapped in their separate rooms.

Thand had become detached since the day of the humiliating training session. He had even refused to help with preparations for the trip back to Elingale.

Just like the storm that was raging outside, his anger and resentment continued to build. He thought about the humiliation he had suffered when Queen Twila implied that he wasn't good enough for her daughter. Cayman was belittling and had purposely injured him during the training sessions. Then there was Sharman, who hadn't stood up for him during any of this.

By late afternoon on the second day, the storm had subsided; however, the high swells continued to heave the ship. The captain hadn't changed the order to stay below deck, but Thand had to get out of his claustrophobic room. Waiting until dusk, he went topside.

The air was brisk and rejuvenating. *Strange*, he thought, *it's always like this after a big storm.* Destruction could lie all about, but the sky would be beautiful and the air would be fresh and clean.

A bluish-orange light caught his eye. Three sailors had built a warming fire in an old cask. This practice of burning off the residual alcohol in a rum barrel had been banned by the captain for obvious reasons. Fire aboard a ship was everyone's greatest fear. However, it seemed these men thought the rules didn't apply to them. Their slurred voices implied that they had emptied the bottom of the barrel before setting it ablaze.

One of the men saw Thand, then stood and waved him over. "Thand," the man called in a sloppy voice. "Over here." The sailor took a step forward, but lost his balance. He grabbed the barrel for support, but instead pulled it over on himself. The flaming liquid set him on fire and then spread across the deck. The others stared, frozen in horror.

Thand instantly removed his shirt and ran toward the screaming man. *Smother the flames; smother the flames.* Wrapping the burning man with his shirt, he pushed him to the deck and rolled. The cry of pain was worse than anything Thand had ever heard. The sailor flailed as they rolled away from the fire, but when his burning clothes had finally been smothered, the man wasn't breathing.

Thand removed the burnt remains of the shirt to inspect the sailor's injuries. He clutched his stomach; the man's face was charred and blistered, and his skin was black and leathery.

"Fire!" someone screamed. The burning alcohol had spread across the deck and started a secondary fire that was growing rapidly. The quarterdeck watchman began ringing the ship's bell wildly. Men came running from everywhere to form a bucket brigade.

"Stop this fire or we'll all die," Thand shouted at the men who were staring at their friend. Thand turned away, stepped into the bucket line, and helped pass the water pails from man to man.

Blistering yellow patches had formed on Thand's forearm. "Are you okay?" A sailor asked as he passed the water pail. Thand didn't respond but reached for the next bucket. The rough, hemprope handles shredded the burnt skin on his hand. The pain was excruciating, but Thand focused on the fire.

Twenty minutes later, the battle was over. He stood there dazed, not sure what to do next. Then he heard a distinct voice.

"Your hands are raw and bleeding. I can't tell how badly you've been burned because you're covered in soot. Let me take you to the ship's doctor."

"Leave me alone, Cayman! I don't need your help."

"Can't you turn off the anger for one minute?" Cayman bristled. "You need a doctor. If dat hand gets infected, you could lose it. I've seen it happen. Please, come go with me."

Thand ignored his pleas and began to walk toward the gangway, but the pulsing ache in his hand paralyzed him. The earlier surge of adrenaline was gone, and now his heart seemed to be pumping pure pain.

The princess was standing in front of the passageway door, having only witnessed the final minutes of the bucket brigade. She saw Thand sway, then ran over and reached out to steady him.

"Are you okay?" She frowned as she looked him over. "No. Your hand is burnt, seriously burnt. Let me take you to the ship's doctor."

Before Thand could protest, she locked her arm around his good one and guided him toward the medical facility. The searing pain intensified as he stumbled along.

More than a few sailors had received burns and cuts. They stood in line, waiting for medical treatment. Princess Sharman ignored the queue and walked Thand to the front. The first man in line stepped back and said, "Stand in front of me. It will be an honor." Another sailor called out, "Thand, you're a hero!" The touch of the princess was comforting. Her caress worked like a painkiller.

Princess Sharman guided Thand into the sick bay. The doctor looked at his burns and wrinkled his brow. "This is bad, but not life-threatening. You'll definitely have a lot of pain for the next few days," he said as he treated the burn with ointment. After wrapping the injury in a white linen bandage, he handed Sharman a small packet that contained a light green powder.

"Here, give him this. This will speed the healing and help ease the pain."

She thanked the doctor and then slid the packet under her belt. Thand leaned heavily on Sharman as she guided him down the gangway and into his room.

He sat on the edge of his bunk with his head practically touching his knees.

She poured a cup of water from a nearby pitcher and then stirred in the powder. The aroma of peppermint filled the room. "Drink this, then lie down."

He did as he was told. "Thank you," he whispered and then drifted off.

Chapter 44

PRINCESS SHARMAN STROKED Thand's head gently with a cool cloth. He was asleep now, out of pain. *What would I do if I lost him?*

She laid a blanket over him and spoke softly. "We shouldn't have let this quarrel continue. Too much time has been lost to anger. The flirting and attention seeking was wrong, I know. But I was trying to get you to pay more attention to me and less time thinking about that feather. We should have talked instead of fought."

When his breathing became deep, she kissed his forehead and went to her room. She crawled into bed feeling like she could sleep for a thousand years. But just before dawn, another dream came to her.

Once again the vision began with the faraway noise and a pirate bursting through her cabin door. She stood by the window and showed no fear. Thand would show up at any moment. The man held a cutlass in one hand and advanced on her. One eye was bloodshot, the other milky white. "Don't worry, my pretty one. I'll protect you," he said in a chilling voice.

The intruder moved closer, knife pointed at her chest. He smelled like rotted seaweed. Her eyes darted around the room.

Where's Thand? When the cutthroat got close, he threw down his knife and lunged for her. At the last moment, she sidestepped, grabbed him by the shoulders, and used the momentum to throw him through the window. Strangely, there wasn't a splash.

She ran to the window and looked down into the water, but the pirate wasn't there. Instead, Uncle Warmund was bobbing in the water. "Stop worrying about me," he shouted. "I'm fine." Then, with a single wave of his hand, he slipped silently below the water.

A new noise came from the hallway. She spun, grabbed the knife, and crouched in a fighting position. The door swung open. Thand was standing there, wearing his padded training vest and holding a white feather in his hand. "Don't worry. I'll make everything okay."

When she awoke from the dream, she sat up and pulled her knees to her chest. What were the meanings of these nightmares? What did this last vision mean? Should she stop looking her uncle? Was Thand really going to save everyone with his feather?

Chapter 45

ESCHON WAS UP at first light. Today Enunciation would actually teach him a conjuration, not just talk about it. He had been thinking about it all night. Which spell would he learn? Something powerful and devastating, he hoped.

Suddenly, he was not interested in learning a new spell. He missed his family. All these exciting things happening, and there was no one to share it with. *How can I do this without my brother? I've never accomplished anything important without him being there to encourage me.* He wanted to go back and set things right. Then he reminded himself that his brother had told him to get out. *What caused this change?*

As he got dressed, an idea came to mind that would distract him from his troubles. The plan was a little deceitful, but he would go to the kitchen and ask for some fresh bread, knowing that it wouldn't be ready at this hour. A cute, willowy teenage girl named Debee had been added to the cook staff recently. She was short and slender, which meant that they were the same size. He was fascinated.

He entered the kitchen while the girl's back was to him. Ringlets of straw-colored hair dropped to her shoulders.

He walked toward her and said, "Good morning."

She jumped and yelped at the same time. Her hand flew up, creating an instant cloud of flour.

"I'm sorry. I didn't mean to startle you," Eschon said, begging forgiveness.

Debee made a quick recovery. She looked down at her shoes, twisted a strand of her flaxen hair, and said, "That's okay. It's just that I'm usually here by myself at this time of day."

Eschon smiled. "I know."

"The bread won't be ready for at least another hour," she said with a mischievous twinkle in her eyes. "Unless you help me."

He moved next to her and picked up a hunk of dough. "Show me what to do."

She bumped her hip into his and said, "You're so helpful. Maybe you need to come down here more."

Her reaction eased his anxiety. "Today is going to be exciting. Enunciation is helping me create an awesome spell."

"I hope you choose a love spell. They can be very useful."

Eschon blushed, and the small talk continued until five loaves were formed. After the bread was put in the oven, Eschon picked up a knife and began to peel apples for a pie.

"Who taught you to do these things?" she said in a cheerful voice.

"My—"

A house servant burst in the room, startling them.

"You should report to the tower immediately. Your tardiness has been noted by the wizard."

A pinched expression crossed Eschon's face. *Had that much time passed?*

He reclaimed his composure and displayed a wide grin. "It seems the wizard can't continue without me. I'm an important part of his work, you know. I'll return when I can."

Eschon arrived in the tower breathing hard, ready to be wizardly. Enunciation pointed to a pile of dried leaves and said, "Start there."

The proud, up-and-coming, young wizard spent the morning sitting in the corner, using a mortar and pestle to crush herbs into powder. By noon, his wrist hurt from grinding and twisting—and so did his ego. *What's the big deal calling me away? Anyone could do this.*

The afternoon was more to his liking. Eschon sat on a stool, back straight, both hands folded in his lap.

Enunciation looked into his eyes sincerely. "Remember what I said earlier: Being a wizard is a vocation, like a teacher or a man of medicine. You must dedicate yourself to learning and practicing your craft."

Here comes the lecture, he thought. *He's heard about Debee.*

Enunciation spun his finger in a circle. "Energy is all around us. It is what holds the universe together. Magic is the art of consciously focusing and controlling elemental energy. Through prudent effort, we use this force to shape things."

The wizard's hands moved upward. "The magician's job is to lift up and focus this energy, then release it to produce the right effect. Let's start by saying these words:

"To the left and right of me, above and below me, I awaken the spirit of nature and the magic within me.'"

Eschon closed his eyes, as if he were saying a vow, and repeated the words.

"Good. Now let's begin. I have chosen an uncomplicated repulse spell. It's designed to block low-velocity, light-weight objects. For example, this enchantment would repel a stone, but not a spear. It would push a person away, but not knock them down. What elements do you think we'll need to make the spell?"

"The element air to propel. And I would add earth to act as a screen from the person I was trying to resist. Maybe get dirt in their eyes so I could run."

"That's a good combination. I hadn't thought about adding the earth element."

As the days progressed, the spells grew more complicated. Some were even dangerous, but Enunciation didn't seem concerned. Eschon was smart and confident. He was making it clear that he could deal with the rigor of becoming a wizard.

The next afternoon, when the young apprentice was distilling water, Enunciation walked into the room humming a happy tune. Eschon looked up, wondering if this was good or bad since the wizard was usually as quiet as a cadaver.

The melody ended. "I'll need you to be up and ready to work before sunrise."

Eschon's face sagged. *More bloodworms.*

"I need you at the cave, first light." Enunciation paused for a beat. "It's time you learn to fly Drächenrød."

Chapter 46

*E*SCHON ROLLED OUT of bed several hours before dawn, lit a candle, and grabbed his notes. *Fly! No wonder I can't sleep.* Practice time was over, and today would be his first solo flight.

Dragons change direction only by verbal command, he reminded himself. *Their skin is too thick to feel nudges from the rider.*

He had spent many hours studying the ancient language of the dragons and had burned into his memory the basic flying commands. But still, he felt the need to review them one more time. *Descendit* was down, and *tardi* was slow. He doubted if he needed to use the word *ocius*, because fast seemed to be the only speed that Drächenrød knew.

Drächenrød wore a customized headpiece, with reins attached. It was designed to help the rider stay balanced, and not meant to guide the dragon's direction. Eschon snickered as he imagined what it would take to bridle Drächenrød. Forcing her to open her mouth while attaching an uncomfortable apparatus would cost you your hands and maybe your head. But if somehow you suc-ceeded in placing the bit in her mouth, one blast of dragon fire would incinerate it.

Flight would be the easiest part, since that was Drächenrød's job. But staying balanced on her back was his responsibility and foremost concern. Head up and chin forward. Shoulders straight and level. Back straight, but not stiff. Discovering the center of gravity on a dragon wasn't easy, but falling thousands of feet to the ground was a good incentive to learn.

When Eschon and Enunciation arrived at the cave, Drächenrød was already out, lounging on the ground and picking her teeth with her front claw. The bones of an animal lay strewn before her.

The scene reminded Eschon that he hadn't eaten this morning. Maybe that was the reason for the slight headache. He walked toward the dragon hesitantly, still fighting a desire to flee. He scolded himself, *You can't show fear in front of Drächenrød.*

Eschon's mouth was dry and his palms were clammy when he climbed onto the saddle. *It's not fear of the dragon, but fear of failure,* he told himself. The muscles in his hands twitched when he took the reins from Enunciation.

"Don't worry. She'll get you into the air," Enunciation said in a calm voice. "It's like riding a gigantic horse—except it gets smoother once you leave the ground. Now, go."

In three thunderous steps Drächenrød was standing at the edge of the cliff. She raised her head and looked up into the sky, then lit up the morning mist with the burst of fire. Eschon feared that he had done something to upset the beast. Then, like she had sensed his misgivings, she turned and looked at him to make sure he was seated properly.

Eschon swallowed hard, then took a deep breath, letting it out slowly. He rebalanced himself and then called, "*Volare,*" meaning *fly.*

With a swift downbeat of her wings, Drächenrød leaped into the sky and headed for the clouds like a homesick angel. The acceleration was breathtaking. The castle was shrinking by the second, and Eschon let out a war whoop that could likely be heard by everyone in the valley.

A few minutes into flight, Drächenrød saw a deer and plummeted like a falling star. Eschon screamed, "Up, up, surge, surge!" Thirty feet above the ground, the dragon flared her wings as the animal ran into the forest, protected by the tree canopy. They flew across the treetops in a blur, and then regained altitude.

His heart was racing, nearly exploding, from the experience. This was the first trial in commanding the dragon, and he wasn't sure who had won. After an hour of flying, they looped back toward the castle. Enunciation was waiting for them when they landed. "I see you both came back at the same time. That's good. You'll do it again tomorrow."

Most of the flying took place at dusk or dawn, but a few late evening flights were made so Eschon could learn to fly in total darkness. This turned into his favorite type of flying. There was no depth perception, so the fear of heights went away. Usually, he didn't know what was happening until he felt it in his stomach.

A storm had rolled in after dinner, so there would be no flying. Eschon stood by the window and looked out at the lightning flashes. He missed his mother and wished that Thand was here with him. He thought about his friends in the castle. What would the princess, Oden, and Cayman think if they could see him flying the dragon solo? A lightning strike silhouetted a mountain peak. It reminded him of the Black Storm at Elingale. *Where's Baylock? What's his plan?*

Eschon awoke to a bright new morning. He dressed quickly and headed toward the kitchen with Debee on his mind. As he started to descend the staircase, a messenger came running toward him. "Wait, wait. Enunciation needs you in the tower. Right now. A hawker pigeon arrived."

Chapter 47

BAYLOCK GAVE A rare smile as he watched the men work. He now had his own pirate crew—something even he couldn't have imagined when he was running down the escape tunnel in Lapis Lazuli. *Hah! If only my spiteful father could see this, he might take back some of his hurtful words.*

Captain Tiger had surprised Baylock and the crew by being a good captain. He understood the waves and the wind, the stars and the men. All parts of the ship were maintained in shipshape condition. But his chin-up, stiff posture that made him look like a walking beanpole also made him prone to falling. They took to calling him Captain Clumsy, and side bets were made on how many times a day he would stumble. But standing on the quarterdeck, commanding the ship, he was faultless.

The men lived on board the ship even though most of the time they were anchored a short row from Skull Island. Just the sight of the carved rock-skull unnerved many of the sailors. Sedgley reinforced their fears by telling stories of the two-step viper, the clapping spiked plants, and the awful spider named Mactabilis. A quick but painful death would be the reward for anyone defying the order to stay aboard.

The days went quickly. Sedgley and Captain Clumsy worked

together to train the men to seize a ship without actually destroying it. They learned to launch a longboat with as many men as possible and to row silently up to the victim's ship, attach a rope ladder, and board noiselessly. They became proficient in the use of grapple hooks and cable lines, as well as running across a gangplank with weapons drawn.

Baylock wanted no one to doubt the mission of his ship so he renamed it the *Conquest*. He knew that sailors considered it bad luck to change a boat's name, even if it was something as silly as *Seas the Day*. He didn't care what they thought, and Captain Tiger's fear of the magician kept him from objecting to the change.

Baylock wanted a solid crew that could be trusted and that wouldn't question his intent. As a reward for their pledge, he promised to build the men permanent living quarters on a nearby atoll. It would be a pirate's haven where they could do whatever they wished. All the men shouted their approval, but Baylock knew some would wish to go back to their families after a few months. He couldn't allow anyone who had knowledge of his plan, or familiarity with Skull Island, to go back to Whistlers Key and talk. Sedgley was told to question each crewman separately and compile a secret list of anyone who had reservations about a long-term commitment. The next day, the men who had issues were told they would be allowed to see inside the rock, to tour the Cranium. They loaded into Baylock's smaller sailboat and headed for the island. But instead of sailing into the mouth of the Skull, they were taken to the far side of the island and left to wander. Baylock was certain that these men would never live to see another sunrise.

The loss of several men did not go unnoticed, but fear that they might be next kept the sailors from rebelling. When Sedgley was asked how they were expected to man the guns with fewer men, he replied, "Cannon fire is not needed. Baylock will provide protection using his magic. For those of you who are skeptical, just remember the magician's display of power on the docks of Whistlers Key."

That night the men were given extra rations of grog, and then, at the height of their celebration, Baylock and Sedgley came aboard. They went to Captain Tiger's cabin and reviewed their strategy. At sunrise they would sail for Lapis Lazuli.

Chapter 48

THE *TRIDENT SEAS* dropped its anchor in the crystal-clear waters of Lapis Lazuli. Thand, Sharman, and Cayman were in the first longboat with Oden. Once on shore, it was only a ten-minute walk to the village of Elingale.

Thand felt miraculously better. Whatever was in that powder had really worked. Without waiting for the longboat to land completely, Thand hopped over the side, into the shallow water, and splashed ashore. Then, bounding across the sand, he started up the trail to Elingale. He wavered at the spot where he had found the Kookachoo feather and then took off running toward his house.

Cayman helped the princess out of the boat and raised an eyebrow. "Looks like nothing's changed."

Thand's mother, Grace, was in the front yard tending her flowers when she heard her name called. She stood up and clasped her hands to her chest. Thand ran over, picked her up, and swung in a circle. He set her down, then noticed her forehead. "How did you get that scar, Mother?"

"I'm not sure, other than it happened just after you left. I remember waving goodbye and then turning to come inside. The next thing I recall, Treelore was leaning over me dabbing my head with one of her wonderfully smelling ointments. I'm fine now. Don't be troubled."

His eyes narrowed. "I knew it wasn't a good idea to leave you alone. Eschon should have stayed behind."

Her eyes widened. "I thought you were happy to have your brother along. Where is he?"

Thand went over to his satchel and took out Eschon's letter.

"Here, he wrote this for you. It explains why he's not here. Don't worry, he's fine. But a lot has changed since we left home."

She began wringing her hands. "Like what? And what has happened to your hair? It's been scorched. And look—your arm and hand. What do you have to tell me?"

The others walked up before he could elaborate. Princess Sharman called out to his mother excitedly and then embraced her. Oden was next with a bear hug and a kiss, while Cayman stood back from the circle and observed the family reunion. He looked on with a warm smile.

There was an uncomfortable pause where Thand should have introduced Cayman. Instead of being good-mannered, he chewed on his lip, looking toward the front door. The princess cleared her throat and presented Cayman to Grace.

Grace frowned at her son for his rudeness. Then she smiled warmly at their new guest and kissed him on the cheek. Cayman stiffened; clearly this display of friendliness was foreign. "It's okay a chara," she whispered in his ear. "I kiss all the men." He laughed and then relaxed.

Grace turned toward Thand and, in a kind voice, said, "My, you have a way of finding the most interesting friends."

"Cayman has had a very fascinating life. I'm sure he would like to tell you about it."

Cayman didn't need to be prodded and began to speak in

his deep, mellow voice. Thand used the distraction to slip into the house. He hurried to his bedroom, put his sweaty hands on the floor, and looked under the bed. *Good*, he sighed. Dust had accumulated on the floor, and the straw he'd placed between the floorboards was still standing. Stepping outside, he returned to the group.

Grace cupped her elbow with one hand while tapping her lip with a finger. "I'm curious to know about that scar on your leg. What caused—oh! There you are, son. I must tell you before I forget. Treelore has been looking for you. She's come here every day hoping to find you. It's important, she said. And she asked me to let her know the minute you came home."

Just then, the local healer, Treelore, came running up the hill, waving her arms. A tall, thin wood nymph came to mind. She wore a woven circlet of honeysuckle on her head, and a trumpet vine hung around her neck. Elingale had benefited greatly from her curative skills, and after she had learned to read, her healing skills had improved enormously. As her reputation spread, people started coming to Elingale from other islands, seeking her advice.

"Oh, Thand, I'm so glad to see you," she said in a panting voice. "I have something really important to tell you. Can we go inside?"

She looked at Cayman, then back to Thand, and whispered, "Too many ears."

Thand was pleased by her exclusion of Cayman. He pointed to the door and waited as she brushed by. She didn't wear shoes and walked so lightly that it seemed her feet didn't touch the ground.

Once inside, she grabbed his hand, then looked at the burn. "I can heal that. Come see me tonight."

Thand's eyebrows rose.

"No, it's just that we'll be alone. Oh, I mean that I don't like anyone to know my technique." She took a deep breath "Maybe I should just fix it now. Is that all right?"

"Why are you here, Treelore?"

She reached into the pouch on her belt and removed a moist cloth. "Give me your hand. This is for the pain. You still need to see me. Okay?"

"Ouch! I thought this made the pain go away?"

"Jeez, give it a minute. Now, where was I? Oh yeah. Yesterday a man and his son arrived from Raintree Island. The father, a brawny guy—but lovely man, by the way—said someone with a pointed beard had shown the young boy a book."

Pointed beard! he thought. *I'm not going to like this story.*

Treelore continued. "The book had a picture of an exotic bird that the boy said—I'm not sure how he knew—looked like the Kookachoo Bird. He said—he could still talk then—that he had heard rumors of the bird, but had never actually seen it."

Thand was accustomed to Treelore's cadence, but her message concerned him. He began to pace and chew on his bottom lip.

"The bearded man didn't seem happy," she continued. "And he sprinkled the boy with some kind of dust—I don't know what kind—then spoke some words—I'm not sure which. Ever since, the boy hasn't been able to speak."

Already, Thand was thinking that the description, as well as the action, fit.

"It sounds like some type of magic—a spell maybe. If you can't help him, then I'll need to contact Enunciation. He'll lend a hand."

"Baylock! It sounds like Baylock is back."

"Is that a problem?" Treelore asked, fidgeting her braided neckband. "I thought he was gone for good."

Thand's fingers went cold. *Has he learned that I have the Kookachoo Bird's feather?*

Oden stuck his head in the doorway and reminded him that they needed to go to Creedy's mansion to start their search.

"Why don't you and Cayman go? Take Sharman, too," Thand said. "I'll stay here with my mother. I'm sure she has a million questions about Eschon."

Oden tilted his head questioningly. "Sharman?"

"You know who I mean. It was a slip," Thand said irritably.

"Okay, but no one knows that place better than you. And besides, the princess refuses to go back there. The memory of her time in his dungeon is something she'd rather not relive."

"I don't like that place either. Do you know how many times I received the whip?"

Oden frowned. "Did you hit your head during that storm? You don't seem interested in finding the assassin?"

The sooner I go the quicker I return. A false smile crossed Thand's face. "Maybe I did. Of course I am."

When they arrived at the front door of Creedy's former home, Cayman let out a whistle. "This guy wasn't lying when he told me he was rich. Maybe I shoulda taken his offer."

Oden gave him a hard stare before saying, "I know there's a secret passage leading out of his bedroom. He used it when we tried to arrest him. It almost worked. But lucky for us, Eschon was waiting for him outside in the tree."

"You mean Eschon's Last Stand at the Oak Tree?" Thand chuckled.

A slight smile crossed Oden's face. "Is that what you call it? I remember Eschon jumping out of the tree onto Creedy's horse and knocking him to the ground. Creedy was screaming like a banshee when I got there. He thought his leg was broken."

Thand made a chopping motion. "I wish Eschon had broken Baylock's neck."

"Enough. You check out that wardrobe, and I'll start looking behind the pictures and furniture. Cayman, start in the front room."

Thand opened the closet door and pushed some clothes aside. He gave the closet a quick scan, hoping to find another bag of gold. Bending and squatting, high and low, he poked around. But he found nothing of interest. Backing out, he noticed a tarnished silver key hanging on the rear wall. Wondering why a door key would be inside, he examined the keyhole on the backside of the door. A few inches below the regular lock was a small oblong hole. He grabbed the key, inserted it, and then twisted. Nothing. He turned it to the left. There was soft resistance, so he tried harder. Then, *snap*! The key broke in half.

"Bedamn!" He reached down to pick up the broken key and felt a cold draft on his hand. He turned around to see that a four-foot wall panel had silently slid open.

Oden went to the closet to ask Thand a question. He looked inside but it was empty. Just as he was about to turn away, Thand called through the trapdoor, "I've found a secret passage. It leads down to the first floor."

Oden smiled and then squeezed through the back of the closet and into a small corridor. The light was dim and the scent of damp earth hung in the air.

Oden reached into a leather pouch and pulled out a rectangular object. It was slightly larger than his hand. He struck it in the palm of his other hand, and immediately, a bluish-green light lit up the space.

Thand's eyes grew big.

"A gift from Enunciation," Oden said with a grin.

He gave the light to Thand and pulled out a second one. They started scanning the wall. After a few probing minutes, the only thing found was the button for unlocking the hidden door. They continued scanning the wall, banging on bricks, and tapping the wooden floor. Soon, Thand grew tired of bumping his sore hand into Oden and moved down to the bottom of the passageway.

At the foot of the stairs, Thand saw a tunnel that led to the barn. *So that's how he escaped the house.* He began searching again and noticed that sand had accumulated along the wall of the second step. *Sand? Why not dirt?* He reached down and picked up a small portion and rolled it between his fingers. This wasn't beach sand. It was too fine, more like the mortar used in between bricks.

Thand's heartbeat quickened. "Oden, I found something interesting down here. There's crumbled mortar on the step. Loose brick maybe?"

Oden hurried down the stairs, then handed Thand a knife. He held the light while Thand inserted the blade between the grout and brick. With a few short, quick movements the brick began to move. Thand wiggled the brick loose and gave it to Oden.

Oden inspected it. "Nothing. Just a simple brick."

"One loose brick? That's not a coincidence," said Thand. He aimed the light into the cavity and saw that a brown piece of paper was tucked in the back. He reached in and pulled it out.

Oden held the light over his shoulder. "What's it say?"

"You know, last year I wouldn't have been able to read this," he replied while unfolding the paper. He squinted in the dim light, then read out loud. "The poison is ready. Five hundred when you give me his name, and one thousand more when the job is completed."

He looked at Oden. A shiver went down his back. "It's signed by Baylock!"

Oden bared his teeth. "That son-of-shade! He paid someone to kill the princess."

Thand scratched the back of his neck. "Yes, but this incriminates Creedy as well. Why would he hint at a clue if he's involved?"

"Baylock's name wasn't coming up in the investigation as a serious suspect. Maybe he wanted us to know that Baylock was the real villain."

Bang. "Ouch!" Cayman stuck his head through the secret door, rubbing his head. "I've been looking everywhere for you. Didn't you hear that cannon shot?"

"What?" Oden seemed startled by the news. "No, sound doesn't carry through the walls."

Thand's mouth went dry. "Baylock! Who else would want to attack Elingale?"

"He wants Princess Sharman," Oden said under his breath.

Chapter 49

BAYLOCK WAS NEARING the island of Lapis Lazuli. The clear morning sun shone bright, but remnants of a two-day storm had left the sea blemished with whitecaps.

The wizard looked across the choppy sea to the west and recalled the long-standing hatred he had for King Treutlen. His cheeks grew hot just thinking about it.

Ten years ago, the king had begun a quest for a new court wizard. Eventually, the search was narrowed down to two people, Baylock and Enunciation. Enunciation's wisdom was admirable, but most thought Baylock's younger age and vitality made him the likely choice.

On the first day of springtide, the two wizards were summoned to the Council Room to hear the king's decision. Enunciation was already seated in front of the king when Baylock entered the chamber. Dressed in black and wearing a red cape, he walked through the entrance way and then paused. Once he was sure everyone was watching him he raised his chin high and then strode toward the monarch.

The two wizards were asked to kneel before their majesty. The king looked down on their faces, letting the silence hang in the air. Then, in a voice for all to hear, he spoke.

"A thorough examination was conducted on the candidates, and their qualifications were studied carefully. At first I thought that this would be a difficult decision, but a review of the information left me with only one choice. Two days ago, I discovered that the Wizard Baylock was creating fiendish incantations and testing them on real people, without their knowledge."

Murmurs rippled through the crowd. The king held up his hand for silence and then looked down on Baylock.

"Some of his victims have died, and others have been disfigured."

Baylock stood and cried, "That's a lie!"

Fast as an eagle strike, the king's guard kicked Baylock in the back of the knees, sending him back to the kneeling position.

"Another word and I'll take your head," growled the guard into his ear.

The king ignored the predictable outburst and turned his attention to the Wizard Enunciation. "You are the wise one. Your past is honorable. Please stand."

Then Enunciation stood and bowed his head. King Treutlen was handed his ceremonial sword, laden with precious jewels. He placed the blade on the wizard's right shoulder and then moved it to his left while saying the words, "I grant you the title of Great Wizard. The designation will be added to your name, and forevermore you will be known formally as the Great Wizard Enunciation."

After the applause died down, the king went on to praise Enunciation as a compassionate wizard who used his powers for the good of other people, without regard for personal gain.

Baylock's face flushed as he listened to the king's words. He was not used to humiliation. It was only the presence of the guards that kept him from jumping up and strangling the king.

King Treutlen turned back to Baylock. "You are the worst

kind of wizard. Lining your pockets with gold seems your only motivation."

The king paused for a moment, then looked out to the gathering. "From this moment on, Baylock is banished from my lands. Imprisonment will be his fate if ever he returns."

Baylock's face turned evil. But before he could protest, the guards yanked him to his feet and dragged him out of the room.

Outside of the castle walls, he vowed to make the king suffer terribly for this disgrace. Then he added Enunciation's name to his revenge list.

Time passed, and then several months ago, Lord Creedy came to him with the task of destroying the Elwin's ability read and write. When Creedy told him that the king's daughter, Sharman, had been their teacher, he realized that an incredible opportunity had been given to him. He could eliminate her and satisfy his need for vengeance, knowing that the pain and guilt of her death would destroy King Treutlen.

But Lord Creedy was afraid of the king's reprisals and refused to be the princess' executioner. However, he agreed to find an assassin for Baylock. The time and place for the execution would be the wizard's decision.

Baylock returned to the task at hand and scanned the horizon. Today he would concentrate on the elusive Kookachoo Bird. It lived somewhere on Lapis Lazuli, so it was just a matter of finding its nesting place. If Thand would show it to him, it would be simple. If not, people were going to get hurt. Either way, he was going to get that feather.

It was just before noon when the lookout yelled, "Land ahead, with ship at anchor."

Baylock grabbed the spyglass, scanned the horizon, and then cursed. "Gotterslamit! Why would there be a ship in Elingale?"

He scanned forward to the bow of the ship, searching for the figurehead. *There. The mythical god, Neptune, holding a three-pronged spear. The Trident Seas.*

"Sedgley, arm the men. That ship belongs to King Treutlen. There could be trouble."

Taking no chances, Baylock uttered the words of his invisibility spell:

"Cloak what they see,

But let me be."

Nothing changed. The crew went about their normal duties, unaware that an invisible dome had encircled the ship. But the wizard knew that anyone looking in the direction of his ship would only see sky and water.

Precise navigation was critical now. The invisibility cloak would burst like a bubble if the magical dome touched *Trident Seas*, but that was just what he wanted. When contact was made, a loud explosion would occur, and then out of thin air, a ship would suddenly appear. The startled enemy would be frightened and confused, making easy prey for his men. But Baylock wanted more than confusion and fear. He needed the *Trident Seas* disabled, so that it could not give chase at a later time. There was a magical solution for that also—his demolish spell.

Quickly, the distance closed on the anchored ship. One hundred yards from the ship, the wizard pointed his middle and index fingers at the *Trident Seas*. A blue-white beam flashed from his fingertips and struck the ship. The center mast exploded and toppled to the deck.

On the *Trident Seas* it looked like a bolt of lightning struck from a cloudless sky. As the mast came crashing down, a warlike ship materialized in front of their eyes. Baylock's trained crew threw grappling hooks and pulled the ships together. Others were more impatient and swung across the ships on a rope, screaming all the way. Then planks were laid between the vessels, and before the sailors had a chance to retrieve their weapons, they were overpowered. Frightened, mystified, and surrounded by enemies, they looked toward the captain's quarter for an answer.

A large, powerful man, dressed in black clothes, was standing where they expected to see their leader. He had dark, slicked-back hair and a neatly trimmed, pointed beard. His intense stare was fear-provoking.

Moments later, Captain Boreas stepped out of the captain's quarter with a flintlock pistol stuck in his back. Sedgley pushed from behind, smiling triumphantly.

Baylock looked at the bewildered captain, then tilted his head back and let out a booming laugh. "How's that for commandeering your ship, Captain? I'd be extremely embarrassed if I were you."

Then he walked up to Boreas and stuck his finger in his chest. "I will destroy you, your ship, and your men if I do not receive complete cooperation." He turned and looked at the frightened sailors. "I will not repeat an order. Anyone who hesitates will be buried on the beach at low tide with just your head visible. Now, do I need to tell you what happens as the tide rises?" Back to Boreas, he barked, "Make sure they cooperate."

The captain's stony face did not flinch, but he acknowledged the threat with a barely perceptible nod.

Sedgley began barking orders, and within moments, the *Trident Seas'* men were herded below deck. The longboats were filled with Baylock's soldiers and lowered to the sea. Twenty minutes later, a complete army was on the beach and ready to fight.

Baylock was the last to come ashore. He climbed out of the boat and scanned the shoreline like a conquering hero. His return to Elingale had been quite spectacular. His encore would be better.

Chapter 50

T HAND JAMMED THE note in his pocket and ran through the hidden passage, emerging inside a barn. Then, dashing past some startled horses and out the barn, he sped toward his house. Ahead, Oden and Cayman, with their longer legs, were already halfway to the house.

Thand lost sight of the other two soon after they crested the hill. Gradually, he slowed to a walk. *Why am I running toward Baylock? He has no idea that Sharman is here. Probably thinks she's dead. No, it's the feather he's after.* His stomach turned at the thought of Baylock with his feather. He had to protect it. Oden and Cayman could look after her.

He took off running again. At the hilltop, Thand could see the backs of his mother and the princess. They were standing behind a tree, looking down toward the village. The king's soldiers, who were supposed to protect Elingale, were being marched into the field at gunpoint. Baylock's other soldiers had encircled the villagers to keep everyone contained. At the center of all of this, Oden and Baylock faced off. Their pointing fingers and body language showed that they were in a heated discussion.

In an effort to avoid detection, Thand sneaked around to the back of the house and entered through the kitchen. He noticed the front door was partially ajar, a sign that his mother didn't plan to be gone long. He rushed into his room, pushed the bed to one side, pulled up the floorboard, and dragged out the box. With fingers shaking, he opened the lid. His cry of relief was so loud he was afraid it had been heard outside. He glanced over his shoulder—all clear. He must hide the feather in a safer place.

He chewed on his bottom lip as a wave of doubt washed over him. He felt like a coward for deserting his friends. But if Baylock got hold of the feather…

Soon they'd understand he was making the right decision. Out in the woods, he would bury the magic feather, and then he'd deal with the barbaric wizard.

He picked up the plume and made one more desperate wish. *If you have any real powers, then protect us from Baylock.* A gleam of light caused him to notice the gold key still lying in the bottom of the box. This simple key had become a symbol of the unique relationship between the princess and him. The key to knowledge, as they called it, was hanging on her neck the first time they met. It was the last thing she gave him before leaving the island. The gesture was a promise that she would return to him.

Now he wasn't so sure about her feelings. His stomach knotted; he scrubbed his hand over his face. An outcry from the village startled him. He checked the doorway—still clear. He crept through the kitchen on the balls of his feet and peeked out the back door. The Kookachoo's feather was tucked under his shirt. The key was in his hand. He hesitated and cursed Baylock for placing him in this spot. *The feather must be saved. They will just have to understand.*

Then, like a thief in the night, he slipped out the back door and dashed to the woods.

The shadows and brushwood helped Thand stay hidden as he

moved through the woods. But just when he thought all was clear, someone shouted, "Stop or I'll shoot." To his left, a ragtag teenager from the wizard's army was pointing a rifle toward him. In one swift motion, Thand reached down, picked up a stone, and hurled it at the boy. The rock hit him on the side of his head. His eyes glazed over and then he tumbled. Thand took off like a deer. Speed, not stealth, was suddenly more important.

He ran like a rabbit, trying to stay hidden amongst the forest plants. At the base of Facetree he stopped and crouched. His heavy breathing made it difficult to listen for any signs that he'd been followed. A dove cooed in the distance—a good sign that he was alone. He moved upward, limb by limb. Then, halfway to the top, he remembered Eschon. He reversed his climb and ran deeper into the woods. Only he would know the new location.

There was a spot where a half-rotted tree trunk was lying on the ground. It would make a good marker, easy to find in the future. He could bury the feather and then roll the log over the hole.

Thand was dizzy and short-winded by the time he found the rotting tree. He dropped to the ground and began shoveling out the loamy earth. How deep? He couldn't have an animal dredging it up.

He heard a twig snap and then the sound of rustling leaves. *Animal? Person?* The sound was drawing closer. He flattened himself behind the log, willing his heart to beat softer.

Chapter 51

Eschon had never seen a hawker pigeon before today. The bird was a creation of Enunciation's genius. The pigeon's homing instincts were combined with the speed and fighting skill of a falcon to make the perfect bird for carrying long-distance messages swiftly.

The note was carried in a capped, leather cylinder attached to the bird's lower leg. Enunciation read the news and passed it to Eschon. "I don't know why they need you to search a house, but it's past time you fly beyond this mountain range."

Eschon rubbed the back of his neck. "I don't know the inside of that house very well. Thand and Oden are the experts. Do I have to go?"

"Yes. It's a command from the king. And you'll have the opportunity to use your navigational skills. And you can bring me back some of that dragon bone."

The night was clear and cold as Eschon walked down the trail toward Drächenrød's cave. Jumping off a cliff, in the middle of the night, on the back of a dragon, seemed like madness. He strived to put aside the worst-case scenarios as he continued to the mouth of the cave. A half moon cast a weak light that blended perfectly with his pallid face.

He stood on the left side of the entrance and rubbed his arm. The acrid smell of the cave had become familiar. This was not practice; he had a mission. After rolling his shoulders to dispel the tension, he called out to Drächenrød. She didn't clear the cave with a blast of fire—that was progress.

The dragon came forward already saddled. He hopped on her back, adjusted the tackle, and maneuvered to the edge of the cliff. "Well girl, I really need your help tonight. Finding an island a hundred miles from here in the dark won't be easy."

Over the last several weeks a bond had formed between Drächenrød and Eschon. They both had learned to trust each other, and she seemed pleased to be flying more often than she had in years. He wasn't sure how he was able to sense it, but he knew Drächenrød was more content now that she had a purpose.

Eschon took a deep breath and let it out slowly. Enunciation had so much confidence in him that he wasn't even there to see him off. He took another deep breath, and then, in a commanding voice, he said, "*Volan.*" The giant dragon sprung into the air like a red grasshopper, unfolded its wings, and began soaring.

Joy, dread, and excitement were tangled up in Eschon's emotions. He was looking forward to seeing his mother and all of his friends, but he didn't know what to expect from Thand. The last encounter with his older brother had gone poorly. Thand's self-centered obsession with the Kookachoo Bird's feather was changing his personality and driving people away. Eschon had no reason to believe anything had changed.

A little after sunrise, Lapis Lazuli came into sight. At least Eschon hoped it was Lapis Lazuli. He'd never seen the island from this height, so he could be anywhere. The directions given to him by Enunciation had been followed without deviation. That is, if he'd pronounced all of the dragon-language words correctly and Drächenrød had understood them properly.

From this height, the island was more beautiful than he had ever imagined. The rocky north mountains were to his left. The village lay to south, and below him was the vast green forest. An azure blue sea surrounded the beach of silvery sand. It all fit; he was home! All of the training had paid off.

There was a cave that Eschon had played in when he was young. It was located on the back side of a hill, invisible from Elingale and in an unpopulated area. It was a perfect spot for concealing the dragon.

Eschon spoke into the dragon's ear, and Drächenrød tilted her wings, spiraling toward the open patch of hillside. She flared her wings and touched down as soft as a butterfly. As it turned out, the cave was smaller than Eschon remembered. But it was still large enough for the dragon to tuck herself in. Drächenrød would be hungry after flying all night. Lucky for her, the smell of dragon was unknown to the wild animals. She wouldn't have to leave the ground for a meal.

It was a little over a mile to Elingale, so Eschon set a fast pace for himself. As he hiked along, it seemed the wild flowers were brighter and the fragrance more pleasant. It was apparent that he was a changed person. Wiser, more mature, and not merely a village boy tagging alongside his big brother.

Soon, the old Creedy mansion was visible on his left. Nothing had changed; yet, everything was different. He had left by ship and returned on a dragon. *I can't get more divergent than that,* he thought.

Eschon crested the hill and looked down to his house. His mother stepped out the front door and into her flower garden. Suddenly, he had no desire to be anywhere else. His throat grew thick. Nothing but family and friends seemed important right now.

Grace looked up and saw him approaching. She ran toward him waving her arms wildly. "Eschon! Eschon! Oh, I've missed you." Suddenly, she stopped and looked around. Her face turned pale. "But you couldn't come at a worse time. Quickly, you must get inside or hide in the woods until this is over."

His euphoric mood instantly evaporated. "What are you talking about?" Looking down to the grotto, he could see Oden, Cayman, and a tall, powerfully built man talking. It didn't look cordial.

"Is that Baylock? What's this all about? Why are all those men in the village?"

Her eyes darted about. "Stop asking questions. Run before he sees you."

"Who? I'm not running anywhere, Mother. Where's Thand? Why isn't he here with you?"

Grace looked around and then toward the house. "I'm sure he's around here somewhere. He came back with Oden and the other man—Cayman, I think. Oh, and there's Princess Sharman walking down the hill."

Grace put her hand on her son's back and pushed. "Please come inside. I don't want anyone to know you're here."

Eschon went inside, not to avoid danger but to look in his bedroom. He wasn't surprised. The bed was up against the wall. A wood plank was missing from the floor. He knew exactly why his brother wasn't here.

He sighed heavily. "Mother, don't tell anyone you've seen me."

Chapter 52

PRINCESS SHARMAN HAD overheard the conversation with Treelore. The thought that Baylock could callously hurt an innocent, young boy had infuriated her.

Quietly, she walked away from Grace, stopping halfway down the path that led to the grotto. Baylock was a bully, always trying to dominate others and using his magic to get his way. Her lips pressed together in a grimace. His evil deeds were common knowledge in the kingdom, and of course, she had fought against his evil magic in order to restore the Elwins' ability to read.

The more she looked at him, the tighter her chest became. Oden and Cayman were already down in the grotto arguing with Baylock. She decided to join them.

Rushing down the hill, she elbowed her way past Oden just as the wizard grabbed Cayman's dreadlocks and pulled his head back. Suddenly, words were not enough. She lunged toward Baylock's throat. Oden knew what she was about to do, grabbed her arm, and pulled her back.

Baylock took a step back and blinked several times. "Princess Sharman! You're supposed to be dead."

The princess took a deep breath and savored the moment. The shocked look on his face was beyond compare. She shook off Oden's hand. "Well, I'm not. Enunciation's magic has always been stronger than yours."

Baylock's jaw clenched and his face turned purple. The veins in his neck began to throb, and she knew she had struck a blow to his bloated ego. She assailed him again. "You low life! I heard about that young boy on Raintree Island. You make Lord Creedy seem like a nice guy. I didn't think that was possible."

Baylock's hands clenched, then unclenched. "Well, I'm glad you're here. You can tell me everything you know about the Kookachoo Bird."

"I didn't know you were a birdwatcher," she said flippantly. "I'm not, so I won't be any help."

"Oh, you'll be very useful."

A feral growl came from his throat. And then, as quick as a cobra strike, he locked his arm around her neck and put his knife blade to her cheek. The princess let out a scream that could have been heard for a mile. Oden lunged for Baylock, but a fast-acting guard bashed him in the head, knocking him unconscious. Cayman reacted at the same time, but a stomach slam put him on the ground. A kick to his ribs kept him there.

Baylock pressed the blade tighter to her cheek, and a tiny trickle of blood ran down the blade. Through a clenched jaw he said, "See, already, you're useful. I'm sure your boyfriend heard your call and will be here shortly."

The princess squirmed and kicked, then broke away for a second. But Baylock grabbed her shirt, tearing a sleeve in the process.

"Give me some rope," Baylock yelled.

Chapter 53

THAND HELD THE feather and wished he were invisible. His face was pressed against the cold ground, feather clutched to his chest, decaying leaves all around. The crunching noise stopped a few feet short of his log. The sound of hard breathing was just above him. He peeked up and saw the flaring nostrils of his brother's face.

Eschon kicked the log. "What are you doing? Get up. If I didn't know you better, I'd call you a coward. They need you in Elingale. Baylock has shown up."

"I know. That's why I'm hiding the feather. He wants it. He wants the power. I'm sure that's why he's here, but I can't let him have it."

Eschon's voice hardened. "Thand, he knows you're here and will do whatever he needs to find you, including harming the princess, our mother, and the villagers. When are you ever going to see that your family and friends are more important than that feather?"

"But that's why I must protect it. Don't you see? With the power of the feather, I can defeat him and help everyone. Better homes. More food. I can make Elingale like Adrianna Island. You, Mother, and Princess Sharman will all be able to live in comfort."

"Always the same promises. Wealth and power. You sound just like Lord Creedy. Is that who you want to be?"

Thand jumped up, his chin held high. "Don't say that! I'm nothing like him."

"You say you're doing this to help the people you love, but when you're most needed, you run off and leave them to their own fate. The way I see it, power and wealth, not friends or family, seem more important. If that doesn't sound like Lord Creedy, then I'm not your brother."

Heat flushed through Thand's body. "Then maybe you're not my brother! Maybe you're Enunciation's son."

Eschon threw his hands up. "I can't believe what I'm hearing. If that's the way you feel, then have a happy life, Thand. I won't be part of it."

Eschon turned and began walking back toward the village.

The thought of actually losing family focused Thand's thoughts. He began to question himself. Was he really trying to protect the feather, or was that just an excuse to hold on to its power? What power? So far it had only brought misery and scorn. Eschon was furious with him. His relationship with Princess Sharman was terrible. Cayman seemed to hate him. And Oden ignored him. He hadn't been happy since the day he'd found that cursed feather.

A lump formed in his throat. *Is Eschon right? Has greed replaced reason?*

Thand studied the bandage on his hand. His physical health was bad and his mental health, too. He recalled the recent fire on the *Trident Seas*. One moment the sailor was talking with his friends, and the next he was on fire. Now he's gone, with no opportunity to make peace. *What if something like that happened to me? Would I only be remembered as a self-centered fool?*

He pinched the bridge of his nose and closed his eyes. *Wealth.*

What's that? Creedy was rich but never happy. And look how he ended up. Fortune and power means nothing if you don't have loved ones to share it with. Why hadn't I seen this before?

Thand stuck the feather in his shirt and raced down the forest trail. He jumped a fallen log and almost fell. He regained his balance and kept moving. Up ahead, he could see the back of Eschon walking slowly toward home. He yelled to his brother, "Eschon, please wait. I'm sorry."

Eschon kept going, but looked over his shoulder and said, "I'm not interested in any more of your excuses. I've already heard them."

Thand kept running, finally getting close enough to his brother that he could reach out and grab his shoulder. "Stop, please. You're right. I've realized wealth and power means nothing if you don't have loved ones to share it with. How could I have forgotten?"

Eschon stopped and turned toward his brother. "I'll tell you how. Your ambition for power has warped your thinking. You chose to ignore the harm you've done to yourself and others. Your intentions were good at first, but then you've twisted them into selfish reasons. Remember, Enunciation warned that power is corrosive and corruption follows."

Thand bowed his head. "How could I have missed this? Enunciation said to me that we sometimes focus on what we want and lose sight of what we need. I wanted Elingale to become a better place to live, without a whip cracking on our backs. I wanted to lead us to prosperity, to be a hero again. That was a very powerful feeling. It's hard to let go. But you've shown me that I've sacrificed my values for greed and power."

"Finally," Eschon cried. "You finally got it right. A person who admits their mistakes and then has the strength of character to right their wrongs is the mark of a good leader."

Eschon pushed his brother's back forward, "Let's hope we're not too late."

But before they took another step, Thand clamped down on Eschon's shoulder. "Wait. You need to know that we found a note that shows Baylock ordered the princess' assassination."

"Son-of-shade!" Eschon roared. "I never thought he would stoop that low."

Just then, a bone-penetrating scream thundered through the forest.

<h1 style="text-align:center">Chapter 54</h1>

T HAND RACED DOWN the hill and into the crowd with Eschon at his side. Sprawled in the dirt, off to his right, Cayman withered on the ground, clutching his stomach. Oden lay motionless nearby.

Princess Sharman stood facing Baylock, cursing him, spittle flying from the force of her words. Her wrists were tied behind her back, her shirt dirty and torn, and her hair bounced with each word shouted.

"Get me a gag, Sedgley," Baylock roared. "I can't listen to her squawking any longer."

Rushing toward Baylock, Thand yelled, "Stop, you devil! Leave her alone. I have what you want."

Eschon veered away from his brother to examine Oden.

Baylock turned and smiled sadistically, then shoved the princess in front of him as if she were a shield. "Your timing is good. I was just about to start wrecking Elingale to find the Kookachoo Feather. Give it to me and I'll leave. This doesn't have to be messy."

Princess Sharman squirmed against the ropes binding her. She kicked backwards, like a mule. "Don't trust him," she shouted at Thand. "Whatever he says is a lie."

The crowd stepped back and Thand faced off against the

wizard. "Let the villagers return to their houses, and send the soldiers to the ship. Once I know everyone is unharmed, I'll meet you on the beach, with the feather."

Baylock's eyes sparkled. "So, you do have the feather. Excellent! No tricks, now. I can level this village without even getting a headache." He put one arm on the princess' shoulder. "But I'll just take your girlfriend here for safekeeping. I'll release her once I have the feather in my hand."

Sharman turned her head in a futile attempt to bite his hand. Baylock slapped her, but still she yelled, "Don't believe him."

Thand was furious but kept composed. "Stop hurting her, you coward; I'll hand over the feather when your army is back on the ship. Princess, don't resist."

Sedgley looked at Baylock, who nodded approval. And then Sedgley gave the order for the soldiers to return to the boats. Baylock walked down the trail to the beach, shoving the reluctant princess ahead.

Thand turned toward the stunned villagers. "Go to your houses and stay inside. This could turn nasty. I'll explain every-thing when I return with the princess."

As the crowd moved away, Eschon looked up at his big brother. "Oden is still breathing and Cayman might have a broken rib."

The words didn't register with Thand; he was too focused on the next few minutes. When the grotto was empty, Thand walked toward the beach as if he were going to the gallows. The cords on his neck stood out like taught ropes.

Eschon, walking alongside, made an effort to strengthen Thand's resolve. "You're doing the right thing, kin. That feather has brought you nothing but grief."

"It's not the feather that's bothering me. If he harms her in any way, I don't know what I'll do. It will be my fault."

Baylock was leaning up against the bow of a longboat with the princess sitting cross-legged in the sand in front of him. The look of triumph on his face infuriated Thand.

The two brothers walked up to Baylock. Thand ignored the knot in his stomach and removed the white plume from under his shirt. The feather quivered as he held it out. "This is the Kookachoo Bird's feather, but it's not what you think, Baylock."

"Nice try, but I know exactly what it is. The power in that feather is what I need to unleash my spell, my greatest spell."

"And what's that?" asked Eschon flippantly. "Another dark, windy storm?"

The taunt wasn't enough to wipe the smile off of the wizard's face. "No. This spell will give me the ability to control words, which will give me the power to crush people like you."

Eschon snickered. "And you think that feather is going to make that possible?"

Thand pulled the feather from his shirt. Baylock' eyes glazed over, and then, in a lightning strike, he snatched the feather out of Thand's hand. "The last element," he breathed.

"You got what you came for. Now untie her and get out of here," Thand demanded.

Baylock blinked and then looked at Thand with malicious eyes. "Oh, didn't I tell you? She's going with me. I want to be sure that you haven't given me the feather of some goose."

Thand lunged toward Baylock but Eschon held him back.

"You lying coward!" Thand screamed. "You said you would let her go if I gave you the feather."

Baylock smirked. "Well, this isn't the first lie I ever told."

Chapter 55

BAYLOCK'S BETRAYAL WAS the last straw for Eschon. He pushed Thand to the side while raising his right hand:

"To the left and right of me,
Above and below me,
I awaken the spirit of nature, and the magic within me.
Drive off this evil man who stands before me."

The air shimmered, then discharged a shaft of energy, striking Baylock in the chest and knocking him off his feet. Thand's mouth flew open as he witnessed his little brother taking action.

Baylock was momentarily stunned, then stood up and slowly brushed himself off with a laugh. "Well, what have we here? A new magician? A puny new magician who's so arrogant that he would attack a master?"

Baylock's lips pulled back, baring his teeth. He pointed his index finger at Eschon, and a blue bolt shot from his fingertip. Eschon flew across the sand and slammed into a palm tree, as if a spoiled child had thrown a ragdoll against the wall.

Baylock puffed up and said, "That's what a real magician can do."

Eschon wondered why Thand was shaking him. His vision cleared, and then he saw the wizard's back moving across the water toward his ship. He climbed to his feet and brushed himself off. Ignoring Thand, he ran in the other direction.

Thand seemed shocked. He had never seen his brother run from a fight.

Without explaining, Eschon began running like a scared deer. He cut through the woods and past the mansion, finally arriving at the cave. *He's not getting away with this.*

Drächenrød was already outside of the cave waiting quietly, a few charred bones scattered around her. Her excellent sense of awareness had alerted her to Eschon's arrival.

He climbed onto Drächenrød's back and shouted the command for flight. The dragon gave a downward beat of its massive wings, and instantly, they were airborne. Quickly, they gathered speed, made a sharp turn, and whooshed over Elingale just above the treetops.

A number of villagers screamed at the sight of the dragon. Some did not comprehend what they saw, while others recognized Eschon on its back and cheered.

The dragon rider soared toward the water. Trees bent beneath like a passing hurricane. As he crossed the beach, he looked down to see his brother pumping his fist eagerly. *I know you'd rather be doing this but you don't have a dragon.*

Once out to sea, Baylock cut loose the ropes binding the princess. She gasped with relief and then rubbed her wrists and rolled her shoulders. "You're not going to get away with this, Baylock."

He looked at her with cold eyes and sneered. "I already have."

Suddenly, there was a great uproar from the crew. The princess looked up and the wizard spun around. Some sailors hit the deck and covered their heads, while others shrieked with fear.

"Drächenrød!" she shrieked.

She looked down and laughed. Baylock was cowering on the deck.

Eschon roared over the ship on the ferocious red dragon, the draft wreaking havoc on the sails. He ascended quickly, then looped around for a slower pass.

"Release her! Release her, or I'll destroy you and your ship."

Baylock stood up. His arrogance reappeared. A chant was spoken as he raised and then pointed his fingertips at the dragon.

"No!" Sharman screamed, running toward Baylock with her shoulder lowered. She hit him hard, but she bounced off like he was a pillar of stone.

A bright bolt of energy left his fingertips. Blinding white light flashed across the sky and hit Drächenrød. For a moment, nothing could be seen but a huge white sun. Then the light faded; Eschon and the dragon were still there. Just before the bolt struck, the dragon had turned her chest plate into the beam, reflecting the energy harmlessly away. Drächenrød had been around for eons, dealing with mad wizards. This was nothing new. But the assault on Drächenrød provoked her anger. She made a sharp, tight circle and then passed over the ship, shooting a torrent of flames.

Princess Sharman dove for the deck, covering her head. When the dragon had passed, she peeked out from under her hands and saw the back of the ship on fire. In the midst of the confusion, she jumped to her feet and scrambled up the main mast. Baylock was too concerned with himself to notice.

Standing at the very top of the ship, gasping for breath, she waved her arms and shouted to Eschon.

Chapter 56

SHARMAN CLIMBED INTO the crow's nest. Amongst the smoke and chaos, she wondered if Eschon had seen her puny gesture. As the fire intensified, waves of heat baked the soles of her feet, and smoke filled her lungs. Time was running out. She gasped for a breath of air, and then everything turned white.

A mysterious gust of wind swept around her and cleared the air. She coughed, then blinked the tears away. Off to her left, she saw the dragon do a barrel roll and swoop toward the ship.

Her back was beginning to feel scorched. The choices had narrowed to a hundred foot jump into the water and probable death or cremation. Sharman climbed to the edge of the crow's nest basket, moved her toes to the edge, and shouted once more. Then she took a deep breath and reflected. *I hope you know how to fly that dragon.*

For a moment, time stood still. She blocked out the heat and chaos below and focused on the dragon's flight. She stiffened, and then a second before the dragon swept by, she made a leap of faith.

The world became soundless as she plummeted toward the ocean. Her body seemed weightless. *I'm falling too fast. The timing is wrong. I'm going to die!*

Suddenly, a jerk on the back of her shirt wrenched her upward, and her feet flew backward. A shriek of happiness flew from her lips as she realized that Eschon did know how to fly the dragon. *I've been snatched from a crushing death.*

When the trembling subsided, she looked down at the ocean flashing below, and then she wondered if this was another dream. Their speed slowed, and her feet began to dangle below her.

Rrrip. Her heart skipped a beat. The dragon's talon had torn holes in her shirt, and the up-and-down motion was making it worse. They were still a mile offshore—too far for her swimming ability. In an effort to relieve the pressure on her clothes, she stretched her hands above her head and grabbed hold of the scaly, red dragon claws. Her shoulders felt like they were on fire, and her wrists were already aching from the vicious way her arms had been tied. Numbness began to spread through her upper body. Her fingers began to lose their gripping power.

"Hurry!" she screamed.

Chapter 57

STANDING ON THE beach, Thand heard a triumphant screech from the dragon. His heart started beating again. "Unbelievable!" he cried as oxygen flowed back to his head. "Like an eagle snatching a fish out of water."

The princess was safely away from the boat, but could she hold on? She was attached to the dragon by the top of her shirt, and she swayed precariously in the wind. Sweat began to form above his lip. It was obvious she was struggling to hold on.

A few flaps later and they were almost to the beach. Suddenly, the princess' grip was gone, and she slipped from the dragon's claws. Thand took off running in a futile effort to catch her. She hit where the surf and sand met. When Thand got to her, she was laying on her back, staring at the sky, with a huge smile on her face. He dove into the sand beside her, wrapped his arm around her waist, and started kissing her just as a wave washed over them. They sat up laughing and coughing and continued to embrace.

Abruptly, the wind picked up, and a dark cloud blotted out the sun. About twenty feet above the ground, the red dragon back-flapped her massive wings to slow down.

Eschon yelled from above, "Never mind, I have my answer."

Drächenrød beat her leathery wings, and they climbed back into the sky, circled once, and then sped back toward the ship.

After the next wave rolled over them, they stood. Thand held the princess at arm's length and anxiously spoke, "I thought I would never see you again. I've been such a fool. Please, please forgive me."

They began a slow walk back to Elingale. Sharman chided, "You've certainly been a dunce lately. Your obsession with that stupid feather had really turned you into someone I would rather not know. But on the *Trident Seas* I saw the old Thand ignore danger and try to rescue a sailor, with no thought for his own safety."

They walked past the spot where Thand had found the feather, but he didn't point it out.

Sharman continued, her voice sounding a little more conciliatory. "And maybe my behavior wasn't the best either. Then, when I was on Baylock's ship, all of our previous quarreling seemed so petty. So, for my part, it's in the past and forgotten."

Thand pulled her tight to his chest and whispered in her ear, "You're the most amazing person I've ever known. I don't know what I would've done if you hadn't forgiven me. And to think, I almost lost you because of a bird feather."

The princess put her head against his chest. "But in the end, it brought us closer. Maybe the true power of the feather is that it showed us that real wealth is love and trust, not a pile of money."

Thand laughed and straightened up her tattered shirt. "But it would have been nice to learn what the feather's power might do."

"Maybe Baylock will throw it away if it doesn't work. You'll have a second chance to find it."

By now a small group of people surrounded them. Treelore, the impetuous local healer, took the princess' hand and said, "I had the strangest thought when you were on that ship with Baylock. How is your Uncle Warmund?"

Sharman lowered her head, unable to voice an answer.

Cayman stood in the circle, clutching his sore ribs. "My experience with pirates tells me it's not a good ending."

Princess Sharman's head snapped up. "We still don't know, Cayman. I've seen you change from a mean-spirited ruffian to a respectable man. Maybe one of those pirates had second thoughts about killing innocent people. If any one of those men were half as decent as you, then my uncle is still alive. So, until somebody proves me wrong, I'll continue to hope."

Just then, a familiar shadow passed overhead. All faces turned to the sky and watched breathlessly as Eschon guided Drächenrød back to the field. The champion and his dragon glided for a short time and then touched down, impacting the ground no more than a falling leaf.

A few villagers raced into the field, hoping to observe the dragon close up. Thand cautioned the bolder ones to keep their distance. "Drächenrød is unpredictable and would roast you if she felt threatened."

Then Thand ignored his own warning, grabbed Sharman's hand, and ran to meet Eschon. The heat from the dragon and the smell of sulfur still hung in the air. They waited at a reasonably safe distance and watched proudly as Eschon slid down the side of the dragon. The look on Eschon's face was like a victorious general.

"Tell me, what's happening to Baylock's ship?" Thand asked breathlessly.

Eschon frowned. "It won't be a ship much longer, but I did see longboats rowing in every direction."

"What about Baylock?" Cayman insisted. "He's too much of a

coward to go down with the ship. We need to find him. If he's allowed to create a spell that's as powerful as he claimed, then we're doomed."

The princess swallowed hard and clutched Thand's arm. "The next storm he creates could make the Black Storm seem like a spring shower."

Thand's mouth went dry, his forehead wrinkled. He wished he had the power of the feather to help him decide. "You're right, of course. We'll have to make a plan."

"That won't be easy," said Oden. "We don't know where he lives. Maybe Eschon and the dragon can scoop him out of the water."

Thand chewed on his lip, sifting through ideas. Suddenly his fingertips began to tingle and his eyes lit up. He put his warm hands on either side of Sharman's cheeks and kissed her quickly. "He's already beaten! Don't you see?"

"No," gasped the princess. "Ouch. You're squeezing too tight."

Thand let go, but in a rush of words, said, "Baylock was going to destroy Elingale if I didn't give him what he wanted. He got the feather, but I didn't give it freely. If you and Eschon hadn't made me understand that our family is more important, I would still have it."

Confused faces surrounded him, but it was Oden who asked, "And what does that mean?"

"It means he used Princess Sharman to make me give him the feather. In essence, he stole the feather from me. The legend says the power of the feather will be lost if it's stolen or not given away freely. I don't think violence and intimidation are used on willing people."

Eschon pumped his fist into the air. "Yes! He's destroyed the power of the feather by his own actions."

Oden's relief was visible. He looked at the two brothers proudly. "Two heroes. One rescued the Princess, and the other saved Elingale from Baylock's destruction. Not a bad day's work."

While everyone was talking, Thand took the princess' hand and pulled her from the crowd. He looked over his shoulder, and already, Eschon had everyone spellbound with stories of the dragon.

They walked halfway up the hill and stood under the ancient oak tree. Thand dreaded this moment, but it had to be done. He had to know her true feelings. He fumbled around in his pocket, pulled out the golden key, and then placed it in the princess' palm. He squeezed her hand tightly, unsure of her response. She looked at the key and smiled, then put it back in Thand's pocket. Placing her hands on either side of his face, she pressed her warm lips to his. He encircled her with his arms and brazenly returned the kiss.

Epilogue

AFTER SEVERAL DAYS of celebration, Eschon announced that he was going back to Aerie Mountain to continue his work with the Great Wizard Enunciation. "I have a lot I want to accomplish, and Enunciation is the only person who can help. Drächenrød wants to get back to the open spaces and cool air of the mountains. I know some of the villagers will be glad to get rid of the dragon stomping around these fields and eating all the game. Plus, I've made a new friend who I'd like to go back and see."

A pained expression crossed Grace's face when she registered what he'd said. After an uncomfortable pause, she looked in his eyes and said, "I'll give you my blessing, but only if you promise to return often."

Eschon looked at Thand and winked. Then, turning to his mother, he said, "As fast as dragon wings can flap, I'll return."

Sharman and Thand laughed at the twist of words.

Then Oden reminded everyone that it was time to sail back. "The king will be anxious for a report."

Sharman walked over to Oden and took his hand. His eyes narrowed, "I'm not going to like this, am I?"

"I've decided to stay on the island and reopen the school. The happiest times of my life were spent here in Elingale. You are tasked with the job of breaking the news to my parents. Tell them they can come and visit me here."

Oden shook his head. "This isn't going to sit well, especially with your mother. But I'll do as you ask."

Princess Sharman looked at Thand and then back to Oden. "My mother thinks that the Elwins are backward people. Let her come and see what they have accomplished."

Grace was pleased to hear Princess Sharman's news. "Well, I might have lost one son, but I gained a daughter."

The *Trident Seas* sailed on the high tide. There was no crowd to see the ship off. Oden had insisted there be no teary-eyed departure, so only Cayman was standing alone on the beach when the last longboat left the island. He had grown fond of the Elwins and decided to stay in Elingale. Some clever talking on his part had convinced Thand that his knowledge of the outside world would be a valuable asset in the transformation of Elingale.

There was a rustle near the trail, and Treelore stepped from the tree line just as Cayman turned toward the village. His eyebrows rose as she walked toward him. Treelore was taller than he remembered and looked almost fragile. But then he remembered that she was more than capable of taking care of herself. It was rumored that she had magic in her blood.

Treelore radiated with energy. "I heard that you were staying— at least for now—or maybe longer. It's a big island—at least for me—but maybe not for you. I mean, you've been to so many places that it might seem small." She looked at her feet and back up at Cayman. "This may seem bold—I'm normally not like this—but maybe you could use a friend."

Without waiting for a response, she looped her arm around his and said, "I'll be happy to acquaint you with my island."

www.ingramcontent.com/pod-product-compliance
Lightning Source LLC
Chambersburg PA
CBHW070430120726
47910CB00003B/725